PURRFECT GHOST

THE MYSTERIES OF MAX 71

NIC SAINT

D1736156

PURRFECT GHOST

The Mysteries of Max 71

Copyright © 2023 by Nic Saint

Edited by Chereese Graves

www.nicsaint.com

Give feedback on the book at: info@nicsaint.com

facebook.com/nicsaintauthor
@nicsaintauthor

First Edition

Printed in the U.S.A

PURRFECT GHOST

Cats Versus Ghosts

When a vagrant was murdered right around the corner from where we live, I felt that trouble had hit a little too close to home. And then when our local park was being overrun with homeless people, preventing us from engaging in our favorite pastime of cat choir, it soon transpired that both incidents might be connected. But how? Before long, we suspected that something was brewing in our neighborhood, with neighbor turning against neighbor in a vicious feud. At least there was something to look forward to: our first investigation into the presence of a ghost! Now that we had more or less mastered the art of catching thieves and murderers, we were moving into the ghost hunting business.

CHAPTER 1

*H*olly Mitchell checked the big chest of toys in the living room for a sign of her daughter's security blanket. Ruby, who was four, had been crying up a storm all day, wondering where her precious rabbit-shaped blankie could be. She had probably dropped it somewhere, or possibly their teacup Chihuahua Babette had taken the blanket and buried it out in the backyard. But wherever it was, she better find it. Ruby's big brother Sylvester had been trying to comfort his little sister, but to no avail. Without Mr. Longears she simply would not be comforted.

"Here, give her this," said Holly's mom, and surreptitiously handed Holly a blankie that looked almost indistinguishable from the original. "I got it from the same store," she added under her breath. The four of them had gone to the mall that evening, and had just now arrived home.

"I guess it's worth a shot," Holly said, and proceeded to make a big display of 'discovering' Mr. Longears under one of the couch cushions. "Ooh, look who I found!" she cried.

Ruby's face lit up like a Christmas tree, but as she grabbed for her precious toy, she said, "He smells funny!"

"That's because I washed him," Holly explained. "Even rabbits need a bath sometimes."

Ruby gazed up at her with those big eyes of hers, then smiled a gummy smile and proceeded to bury her face into her blankie. "I missed you, Mr. Longears!" she declared solemnly. "Don't run away again!"

"Mission accomplished," Holly told her mom with satisfaction. The mystery of the missing blankie hadn't been solved, but at least Ruby was happy again, and that was all that mattered.

It wasn't always easy to raise two kids on her own, but fortunately she got a lot of help from her mom and dad. After her husband Eric had died in a freak accident four years ago, she suddenly found herself a widow, and the adjustment, coming on top of the grief of Eric's death, had been painful. But somehow they had all managed to find a new normal and adjust as well as they could. Even though the kids still asked about their daddy from time to time, especially Sylvester, who had been four at the time, they didn't seem to have been adversely affected too much. They both did well in school, and Holly tried to make their home as warm and cozy and happy as she could.

"I don't think you should go," her mom now said.

"Why? Can't you babysit them?" she asked.

"No, it's not that. It's just that..." Mom made an ineffectual gesture with her hand. "I don't know. Maybe this is just me being silly, but I've just got a bad feeling about this, you know. Especially since..." She glanced over to where the kids were sitting on the couch, both admiring Mr. Longears.

"It's not going to happen again, Mom," Holly assured her. "Freak accidents are exactly that: freakish in their rarity. It's not going to happen again," she repeated, more to herself than to her mom. It was true that the same thought had entered her mind when her boss had selected her to give a sales presentation to their Boston team. Eric, too, had been on his way to an important presentation when his car suddenly veered off the road and had crashed into a ditch. No other drivers had been on the road that night, and the brakes on his car had functioned perfectly. The insurance company and the police had conducted their investigations, but neither had been able to explain what caused Eric's car to careen off the road like that. And now she would be heading to the same hotel in the same city to give a presentation. If her boss had known about what happened to her husband, maybe he wouldn't have selected her. But then she wasn't the kind of person who liked to discuss her private affairs.

"Okay, so maybe you can tell them that now is not a good time," her mom suggested. "That you need to be with your family right now? Maybe tell them that Ruby is, I don't know, teething?"

Which wasn't a lie, since the last of Ruby's baby teeth had recently started appearing. In that sense she was definitely a latecomer, but according to the dentist it was nothing to worry about.

"If I did that, they'd simply select someone else to give the presentation, Mom."

"So? Is that so bad?"

"It would also put me down a few pegs in the pecking order. Next time a big presentation comes up, they'll think twice about asking me. And before you know it, I'll be gently pushed toward the exit."

"That's a pretty inhumane way to run a company."

"Inhumane or not, they want to know they can always rely on me."

"It's the anniversary of Eric's…" She glanced over to the kids, then whispered, "Well, you know."

"Of course I know, Mom. But if I let Eric's death control my life like that, I'll never go anywhere ever again. Accidents happen, and just because it happened to Eric doesn't mean it will happen to me."

"Maybe you could ask someone to drive you," Mom mused. "Book an Uber, maybe?"

"It's fine. I'll be careful," she promised.

"And call me every hour on the hour to let me know how you're doing." She frowned. "Or maybe we should turn it into a family trip? We could all join you. The kids, me, your dad. You know, we could see the city while you do whatever it is that you have to do, and then we'll meet up at the hotel and have a good time. That way I won't spend the whole weekend worrying about you."

She smiled at her mom. "That's sweet of you, Mom, but it's really not necessary. I'll be all right."

"Who's talking about you? I'll be worried sick, and I'm not even talking about your dad. With his heart condition, he shouldn't be put through the wringer like this."

Holly thought about this. Her mom was right, of course. It was bad enough that Dad had lost his beloved son-in-law. If he ever lost his daughter too, that would be the end of him. But then she knew she couldn't think like that, or she would never venture out of the house again—ever. So instead, she decided to change the topic. "So have you and Dad decided on the big move yet?"

Mom made a throwaway gesture with her hand. "Oh, forget about that. Your dad will never go along with me on that one. If I didn't know any better, I'd say he wants to keep on living in that house forever—until his dying day. I keep telling him that place is much too big for us, and we should sell and move into something smaller. But you know your dad. The man is as stubborn as a mule. He keeps telling me that when you repot a plant there's a good chance that it will die. And so if we repot ourselves, there's always a chance we won't survive."

"People aren't plants, Mom," she pointed out.

"I know that, and you know that, but try telling that to your dad!"

"Anyway, sooner or later you'll have to move. That garden doesn't take care of itself, and neither does the house."

Mom and Dad had bought the big house anticipating they'd raise a big family. And they had. With five kids in the house, at one time it had seemed too small to accommodate them all, especially when they had hit their teens and needed a lot of personal space. But since they had all left, the house definitely was too big to maintain, and even though they had been gently pushing their dad to sell up and move into a comfortable apartment in town, with an elevator and all the comforts he and Mom needed, the man was refusing to budge.

"Until he finally sees the light," said Mom, "I'll have to keep paying Maria to come in twice a week, and Arturio to keep up gardening duties. At least those two are very happy with your dad's stubbornness."

To Holly and her siblings their parents' marriage was the gold standard by which they measured their own relationships. Even after forty years the love and respect they had for each other was still palpable. According to Mom it hadn't always been that way, and shortly after they were married they had hit a rough patch. But as she liked to tell the story they had worked to overcome their differences, and after having raised five kids who now all had kids of their own, their marriage was stronger than ever. Now if only Dad would let go of the old house. Holly understood, though, and secretly didn't want them to sell the place either. After all, there were so many memories there—all happy ones.

Holly and her mother watched for a moment as the kids sat transfixed by the new and improved Mr. Longears, with Ruby giving him a million kisses and Sylvester giving his sister a big protecting cuddle. Then Holly went in search of Babette, who had been barking up a storm in the kitchen. She had almost reached the back door, assuming Babette wanted to be let out of the house—they always locked the pet door when they went out—when she almost stumbled over something lying on the floor. She switched on the light and, as she took a closer look, discovered to her horror that it was a man she had never seen before. And if she wasn't mistaken, the man was very much dead!

CHAPTER 2

*M*ark Cooper watched the hullabaloo going on across the street from his bedroom window. There were a lot of lights flashing and police cars coming and going, and he wondered what was going on. As a retired math teacher, he knew the odds of a tragic event taking place in the same family were slim to none, so a second death taking place in the same family was highly unlikely. Probably the mother had taken a bad fall and had to be taken to the hospital, he thought. Or maybe the dad had suffered a cardiac arrest. He hoped the kids were all right. Even though he didn't like Holly, he wouldn't want to see any harm come to her kids. After all, they couldn't help it if their mom was an annoying so-and-so.

The family had definitely suffered through their share of tragedy, with Eric Mitchell dying a couple of years ago. Though this idea that Holly and Eric had been a dream couple was nonsense, of course. Once he'd passed by their house late at night walking Melvin, and he'd heard the couple engaged in a screaming match that had turned his ears red and had even caused Melvin to look up in alarm.

Young love, he thought at the time. One minute they're crazy about each other, and the next they can drink each other's blood.

According to the scuttlebutt, Eric had died in a road accident. Driven his car into a ditch. Holly had turned from a blushing young bride into a widow overnight, and now, four years on, there was still no sign of a new man in her life. Maybe there would never be one. Some women were like that. They lost the love of their lives and never wanted to remarry again. To be honest, he had also been like that. But then he and Jackie had been together fifty-five years before she passed, which was more than Holly and Eric ever had.

Next to him, Melvin also looked at the house across the street, fascinated by all the bright lights.

"What do you say if we take our walk now, Melvin?" he suggested. He could linger across the road for a while, joining the other rubberneckers and ambulance chasers, and maybe find out what was going on over there. He'd read all about it in tomorrow's paper, of course, or on the *Gazette* website. For he'd already seen that Odelia Kingsley woman arrive, along with her husband Chase, the police detective. As usual, they were accompanied by their cats, which struck him as very strange indeed, but then such was life in Hampton Cove. All the eccentrics seemed to flock there. "Must be something in the water," he told Melvin. And as if he understood what his human was saying, the poodle yapped in agreement.

* * *

MAE WEST WAS JUST on her way back from the dog park, where she had walked her Alsatian, Roger Moore, when she was struck by the presence of all those police cars on her street. When she drew closer, she saw that they had all gathered at the place where the Mitchells lived, though it was probably more accurate to say that Holly Mitchell lived there, since Eric had died a couple of years ago now, in some tragic accident she didn't know the details about, nor did anyone else as far as she knew.

"Now what do we have here?" she asked as she approached. The police had cordoned off the area, so she couldn't actually get close to where the action was, and she joined the other people gawking at the events as they unfolded. She found herself standing next to Mark Cooper. Mark had come out accompanied by his poodle, Melvin, and as the two dogs proceeded to sniff at each other, she and Mark exchanged a greeting. Even though she had never particularly liked Mark, she had always tried to maintain a cordial relationship with the man, if only because they were neighbors and forced to bump into each other on a regular basis, especially since they were both dog owners and met one another in the local dog park every day. All the dog owners on the block were members of the same WhatsApp group and kept in touch that way. But Mark, being one of the more overbearing neighbors she had ever encountered, liked to boss the others around to some extent, something she hated.

Her husband, Julio, had always said about Mark that if he had been a general in the army, his own soldiers would have turned against him and shot him. But since they were merely neighbors and Mark wasn't a general but a retired math teacher, no shootings had occurred so far.

"What's going on?" she asked.

"No idea," said Mark. "It started about an hour ago. First, one police car arrived, then an ambulance, then this whole fleet of police cars. That Kingsley reporter went in with her detective husband, so it must be something big if those two are involved."

Mae knew just what Mark was referring to. Chase Kingsley and his wife were big on handling murder inquiries, of which there had been far too many recently. So if they had gone in, this couldn't be Holly's mom who had stumbled over the dog and taken a nasty tumble.

"Do you think... It's murder?" she asked.

"Has to be," said Mark, "if the Kingsleys are involved. And the Kingsley woman had her cats along with her, so that probably means they'll be here all night, sniffing out clues and generally making a big spectacle of things." He sniffed audibly, and contempt was written all over his features. Not every dog owner hates cats, but Mark sure did. In fact, it wasn't too much to say he abhorred the species with a vengeance and wouldn't have minded if cats became extinct at some point.

"I can't imagine. Murder? Here on our street? But who? And why?"

"Like I said, no idea," Mark confessed, and he sounded disappointed as he said it.

"You don't think... Holly?" asked Mae. Even though she wasn't overly fond of Holly Mitchell, she couldn't help but feel some measure of sympathy for the woman. After the tragedy that had befallen her, she still did her best to give those kids of hers a good upbringing. Her parents had been a big help, of course, especially Holly's mom, who was always there to take care of her grandkids.

"I think it must be the mother," Mark now said. "Maybe they got into a fight and things got out of hand. I just can't see what else it could be," he hastened to add when Mae expressed her shock and dismay at these words.

"I just can't believe it," she said. "I only hope... It's not one of those family tragedies you always hear about. You know, that she first killed her kids and then herself."

Mark's face contorted into a frown. "I hope you're right," he said. "Now that would be a tragedy."

She glanced up at her neighbor. Rumor had it that Mark Cooper had been sweet on Holly for a while. Though he was far too old for the woman, of course. But it had to be said that Holly Mitchell was an attractive woman. Possibly too attractive for a widow. But then she had become a widow at a very young age. They had only been married a few short years when tragedy struck.

Roger Moore was straining at the leash to take a look, and now she saw what had caused him to become restless. The Kingsleys were walking out of the house, accompanied by their cats. Roger Moore barked at the cats, and so did Melvin. The cats looked a little intimidated, she thought. They were a big red cat and a small fluffy beige-gray one. Odd, she thought, that the Kingsley woman wouldn't go anywhere without her cats in tow. Then again, she never went anywhere without Roger Moore, so maybe it wasn't all that odd. Just that people didn't usually take their cats with them. They might be companion animals, but not when you ventured out of the home.

One of their neighbors shouted a question at the passing detective, but Kingsley merely held up his hand. No comment, the gesture seemed to suggest.

"Who died?" she suddenly found herself piping up. But the couple passed by without deigning her with a response. Looked like they'd have to read about it in the paper or see it on their local news. And since Roger Moore had started tugging on his leash, eager to get home and have a bite to eat, she said goodbye to Mark and headed on home. On the way there, she passed Norma Parkman, the butcher's wife, and wondered what the woman had done to her face this time.

* * *

NORMA PARKMAN WONDERED why that Mae West woman was staring at her as if she had something stuck to her face. But then she was used to being gawked at on a regular basis. Most people she met seemed to find her fascinating to look at, and so over the years, she had begun to consider it a compliment. Her husband Mikel always said it was because she didn't look like most people, and so they had to adjust their expectations when they first met her. He said she was exotic and had an interesting face. She knew this to be all too true, for when she looked in the mirror in the morning, she sometimes had to adjust her own expectations too. Then again, it was a tough struggle trying to remain as youthful-looking as she did. Oddly enough, it only seemed to become more difficult as the years passed. At fifty-seven, she some-times felt she was fighting a losing battle, but then Mikel said that was nonsense and she looked every bit as lovely as she had when they first met, back when they were both fresh-faced eighteen-year-olds.

She gave Mike's leash a light yank and wondered why it was always her who had to take the damn pug for a walk and why Mikel was inside watching television while she was out there being bored to tears while Mike took his sweet time to do his business. When she caught sight of the flashing lights and the array of police vehicles parked in front of the Mitchell place, her first thought was that Holly's dad had had another stroke. After that first one he'd had a couple of years ago, it was only a matter of time before he suffered a second one, more debilitating this time and possibly deadly. It was always the way, wasn't it?

She just hoped he hadn't died. Holly had already had her share of heartache over the years. First Eric had died, and then, as a consequence, Eric's own dad had suffered cardiac arrest and had turned into a vegetable, only to die six months to the day his son had died. And then Eric's grief-stricken mother had also died, wilting like a flower, as one of their neighbors had described it. She was a nurse in the hospital where both Eric's parents had been admitted and said it was as clear a death from grief as she had ever seen.

So now Holly only had her own mom and dad left, and if the good Lord took those away as well, that would be terrible.

Oh, life just wasn't fair sometimes, was it? Just look at her. Her last boob job had been botched by that terrible surgeon, and now her left boob was slightly bigger than her right, and not only that, but it hung lower than its cousin. Mikel said he didn't mind, but she sure as heck did. She had already made another appointment at the clinic, but if she had to go under the knife again, it would be her fifth boob job in as many years, and frankly, she was starting to wonder when this would end. And then the girl who'd done her Botox this time must have been asleep on the job, for she had ended up with excruciating pain in her left eye and an eyelid that had refused to remain in place. Almost as if the girl had hit a nerve or something. It was a ghastly sight, and for a whole three days, she had been nervous about waiting on people in the butcher shop, afraid they'd start making comments again behind her back as she knew they always did.

She joined the group of neighbors looking at the scene, and when she saw Chris Goldsworthy, she tiptoed up to him. Chris always knew what was going on in their neighborhood. The man was a veritable fountain of wisdom. Chairman of their local watch committee, he made it his business to be informed. It didn't hurt that he was also drop-dead-gorgeous handsome. He reminded her of Don Johnson, who she always thought aged very well. "What's going on, Chris?" she asked. "Who died?"

"I'm not sure," said Chris, much to her surprise. "I think it must be serious, though, I just saw that detective come and go. Chase Kingsley? And also, the county coroner was in there. Abe Cornwall. So if they were here, it can't just be a heart attack or some accident—someone falling from the stairs or cutting themselves with the kitchen knife." He shook his head decidedly. "I think this just might be..."

She stared at him with a mixture of anticipation and dread. "What?"

He turned to her and lowered his voice. "Murder," he said, and she had the impression he actually took relish in the ghoulish fact.

She shivered. "Murder? But how can that be?"

"Murder happens everywhere, Nonnie," he said, using his favorite name for her, though he always made sure that Mikel didn't hear it, since he would only get jealous. That was the problem with Chris: all women adored him, and all men hated him, exactly because of that fact. "Even on our street."

"Maybe some burglary gone wrong," she suggested, for she simply couldn't imagine one member of Holly's family murdering another member. Holly herself was always so distinguished, so kind and unruffled, in spite of the tragedies that had befallen her. And Holly's mom was just the same. Nice, well-respected people, Charlie and Bethany Williams.

"You're probably right," Chris agreed. "Maybe they caught a burglar, and there was a struggle, and in the process, someone died."

Norma stared intently at the house, hoping to catch sight of either Holly, the kids, or her parents. But nothing. Absolutely nothing.

"I better run on home," she announced.

Chris's lips morphed into a smirk. "To tell Mikel what's going on?"

"Of course not," she said, even though he had guessed right. Whenever she had big news to impart, she couldn't wait to get home and tell her husband. He loved all the gossip from the neighborhood, and she loved supplying it to him. And this was certainly the most exciting gossip they'd had in ages. Not since old Mrs. Rutherford had fallen out with her long-time friend Mrs. Davis, and the two old ladies had engaged in a shouting match that had quickly turned physical, did they have the kind of news that earned the qualification 'shocking.'

She just wished she could ascertain who had died. Now that would be a scoop! But if even Chris Goldsworthy didn't know, she certainly wasn't going to find out any time soon. Unless...

She took out her phone and opened her WhatsApp app to check the dog walkers' group.

"Checking the dog walkers' scuttlebutt?" asked Chris with amusement.

She nodded. Though if Chris didn't know what was going on, chances were the other members of the WhatsApp group wouldn't know either, since he was one of the group's most active members.

"And? Any luck?" he asked.

"Nothing," she said sadly. "Even Mark Cooper doesn't seem to know what's going on, and he lives right across the street."

They both glanced behind them at the Cooper place. The lights were on, but of Mark, there was no trace.

"Too bad," said Chris with a sigh. "I probably won't be able to sleep until I know exactly what's going on. You?"

"Yeah, I'm the same way," she admitted. "Stuff like this keeps me up at night."

"But not Mikel, right?"

"No, not Mikel," she admitted with a smile. Mikel was an excellent sleeper. Her husband fell asleep the moment his head hit the pillow, while she could be tossing and turning all night. Or she would finally nod off, only to be wide awake at three, not able to go back to sleep. It was very annoying, especially since they both had to get up early to open the store. But then that couldn't be helped.

"That's because he's a man with a clear conscience," Chris declared, and it could be her imagination, but he seemed to be looking at her just that little bit more intently as he said it.

"I better run," she said. Mikel had sent her a message, she saw, asking her what was taking her so long. He was the best husband in the world, bar none, but he had the annoying habit of being very jealous. Even if a guy looked at her funnily in the store or paid her a compliment, Mikel could get worked up. Good thing he had the good sense never to act on his emotions, especially with the customers, or they could have kissed their business goodbye a long time ago. But even though he rarely said anything, knowing how much it annoyed her, she could feel it when the temperature in their otherwise cozy living room would drop to zero, and he'd sulk and mope all evening before suddenly doing a full about-face and becoming sweet like a pussy cat, showering her with kisses.

One of those psychological quirks, according to a survey in Cosmo she had once read. When you marry a guy, you take the good with the bad, and after all these years, she knew that every guy came with a flaw of some kind. Even Chris Goldsworthy, the most perfect man she had ever met.

But oh boy, did he come with a major flaw!

CHAPTER 3

*I*t isn't often that Dooley and I have to postpone our trip to join cat choir because some tragedy happened elsewhere. Mostly, murderers like to stick to business hours and make sure we don't have to interrupt our regular schedule to mop up the unfortunate aftermath of their nefarious activities. But today was different. Odelia and Chase had already settled in for the evening and were watching some instructive program on television—*Project Runway* if I'm not mistaken—and Grace had retired to bed for the night, while Dooley and I were just about to step out and join our friends in the park to practice our singing voices when the call came in.

Chase was the one to pick up since he's the designated cop in our pleasant little household. From his demeanor I could tell that something not all that pleasant had taken place. Normally, when in a resting state, Chase is mostly easygoing, warm-hearted, one might even say fun to be around. But when he turns his mind to murder and mayhem, which basically is what his profession revolves around, his brows knit together in a frown, the corners of his lips turn down, and generally, he behaves as if there's been a shooting somewhere, which more often than not there has been.

As it turned out a shooting had, in fact, taken place, and our urgent attention was required.

The body had been found by one Holly Mitchell, who happened to live on Russell Street, which is right around the corner from Harrington Street, where we live.

As we walked over there to ascertain how truthful Mrs. Mitchell's 911 call actually was, Chase gave us some more information to go on. "Body of an unknown male discovered by homeowner Holly Mitchell. Mrs. Mitchell lives alone in the house with her two kids and had her mother over for a visit, something that happens very frequently, when she decided to go into the kitchen to let the dog out. That's when she practically stumbled over the body of this man she had never seen before."

"Could be a vagrant who decided to try his luck through the back door," Odelia suggested.

"Could be," Chase agreed in a noncommittal way that is common with him. As long as he hasn't taken in the scene with his own two eyes and ascertained what could have happened, he's reluctant to commit himself to this explanation or that, or generally put the cart before the horse, so to speak.

In due course we arrived at the address indicated and saw that we weren't exactly the first to arrive. Quite the contrary, in fact, as the coroner was there, an ambulance, but also several police vehicles, with officers cordoning off the area and making sure nobody could pass through and take a look at the unfortunate victim.

We walked into the house, having to hurry up since Chase has very long legs and Odelia is pretty quick off the mark as well, and traversed a cozy-looking living room where an older lady sat on the couch with two kids, accompanied by a younger woman who did not look happy to see us. This was probably Holly Mitchell, the person who had stumbled across the dead man, her mother and two kids.

Odelia and Chase introduced themselves to the woman, who was indeed the lady of the manor, and then we proceeded into the kitchen. The victim still lay where Mrs. Mitchell had found him, and for a few moments, Odelia and Chase studied the body from every angle before finally reaching the conclusion that, "The man is dead." This from Chase, who is a professional at this kind of thing.

"Yeah, looks like it," Odelia agreed, also a professional.

And because all good things come in threes, Abe Cornwall, the county coroner, added his own two cents to the conversation by stating, "He's dead, all right."

"I think the man is dead, Max," Dooley said.

"Yes, we've established that," I said.

We moved closer to the body, and immediately I was struck by the strong body odor the man emitted, and also the terrible state of his clothes, an old pair of stained jeans and an equally stained sweater. Almost as if he had lived on the street for a long time and hadn't seen a shower in a while.

Abe pointed to a crimson spot on the man's chest. "Shot through the heart," he announced. "Twenty-two-caliber gun, most likely. The body was still warm when I got here, so I'd say he died between one and two hours ago."

"How many shots?" asked Chase, who looked all business as he studied the dead man, who was lying on his back.

"One bullet, as far as I can tell," said Abe. "Though I'll send you my report later, once I know more about what happened here."

"I think it's obvious what happened," said Odelia. "Mrs. Mitchell caught this man breaking into her house, and so she shot him. But then she realized she might be in serious trouble, so she decided not to mention the break-in or the shooting and claim she had nothing to do with the man's death at all."

"There's no gun registered in Holly Mitchell's name," said Chase, checking something on his phone.

"That doesn't mean anything," Odelia pointed out. She had crouched down next to the victim. "Any ID?"

"Nothing," said Abe. "So we'll have to find out who he is some other way."

"Mrs. Mitchell claims she's never seen the man before," said a police officer, likely the person who had arrived first on the scene. "She says she walked into her kitchen to let the dog out and almost stumbled over the man."

Odelia shot us a meaningful look, and I knew just what that look meant: talk to the dog! And so we went in search of the dog to interview the creature.

We found the dog in the living room, where it sat huddled on the couch, snug and safe behind its human. As far as I could tell, it was a teacup Chihuahua, which is like a regular Chihuahua, only a lot smaller. The dog didn't seem happy to see us as it burrowed even deeper into the couch when we approached.

"What are these cats doing here?" asked the dog's owner, giving us a curious look, as if she had never seen a cat before in her life. Then again, we often get that look, as people don't usually expect a police officer to be accompanied by two cats. But then Odelia isn't a police officer but a police consultant, and we're not regular cats but Odelia's consultants. So you could say that we're a consultant's consultants and have every right to be present at the crime scene, no matter how odd people will look at us.

"Hi there," I said to the little doggie. But instead of replying, the dog merely stared at us, its tongue sticking out between its lips, giving it a funny look.

"My name is Dooley, and this is Max," said Dooley helpfully. "What is your name?"

But the dog either wasn't aware of its own name, or it wasn't talking. So Dooley and I decided to move into the second play in our playbook. It's something we've picked up from Chase himself.

"You did this, didn't you!" I said, adopting a harsh tone of voice. "You killed that man!"

"Oh, don't listen to my friend," said Dooley. "He's just a little cranky because he hasn't eaten."

"I'm cranky because I hate it when dogs misbehave!" I shouted.

"It's all right," said Dooley. "You can misbehave all you want, Mr. Dog, or is it Mrs. Dog? Or possibly even Miss Dog? I mean, it's your home, you can do whatever you want in here, even murder a trespasser. Because that's what happened, right? This man trespassed, and you killed him?"

"But I didn't kill anyone!" said the dog, proving once again that the good cat, bad cat routine never fails to bring the required result. "He was lying there on the floor, dead, when I first laid eyes on him."

"And who made him that way?" asked Dooley.

"I have no idea!" said the doggie, whimpering slightly and quivering from stem to stern. "You have to believe me, good sirs. I would never cause harm to anyone. I've never even bitten a person in my life."

"You've never bitten anyone?" I asked with a touch of gruffness. "A likely story! Now talk, dog, 'cause you're in a heap of trouble here!"

"What's your name?" asked Dooley.

"Babette," said the dog, eyeing me as if I was the worst cat in history, which maybe I was at that moment. Though I have to say, it felt strangely exhilarating to unleash my inner monster for once. "And I honestly don't know what happened, sirs."

"You've never seen this man before?" asked Dooley in kindly tones.

"Never!" Babette said. "I swear. He's certainly not from around here since all the people on the block have dogs, and they walk them every day, so I know all our neighbors, and this guy was never here."

"You walk every day?" asked Dooley. "Isn't that bad for those short legs of yours?"

"Oh, but I love walking," said the dog fervently. "It's my favorite time of the day when my mistress decides to take me out of the house, and we go down to the dog park. I get to hang out with the other dogs while our humans all shoot the breeze. It's great fun."

"Odd that we've never met," I said. "We hang out at the dog park from time to time."

The doggie's eyes went even wider now. "If we had met, I would definitely remember, Mr. Max. I could never forget a cat like you!"

I had a feeling I'd done my work a little too well and had put the fear of God into this dog. So I now relaxed. "I'm sorry for scaring you," I said. "But like my friend Dooley says, I haven't eaten, and when I'm hungry, I tend to get cranky."

The dog's face broke into a huge smile. "Oh, but I can totally relate. When I don't eat, I also get cranky. Very cranky indeed!"

"You wouldn't... happen to have some leftovers for us, would you?" asked Dooley. "It's just that all this murder business always makes me hungry."

"Me too," I admitted.

"Follow me!" said the dog, having become animated now that she realized we weren't going to bring out the handcuffs and place her under arrest. So we followed her into the kitchen, and she led us straight to her bowl, which contained some delicious-smelling kibble. But before we could dig in, Odelia actually swooped in, scooped up the bowl, and placed it on the kitchen counter!

"Hey!" I said, still holding on to my alternate persona, which I tentatively would have called 'Mad Max.' "What do you think you're doing? We were going to eat that!"

"No, you're not," said Odelia decidedly. "We're guests here, Max, and guests don't go around eating food from their host without first receiving an invitation."

"But she did offer us an invitation," I said, pointing to Babette.

Odelia smiled. "The owner needs to offer an invitation," she clarified, "not the owner's dog."

"A new rule," said Dooley with a touch of sadness. "Always new rules to follow, Max. It does get complicated after a while, doesn't it?"

"It sure does," I said with a sigh.

"Just dig in!" Babette whispered invitingly. "I'll cover for you!"

"Cover for us?" I asked with a frown. But since Babette clearly believed in giving service, she now suddenly jumped up, dug her teeth into Chase's calf, and didn't let go again. It was a funny sight: the dog hung from Chase's leg, her tiny teeth just sharp enough to provide some traction against his jeans but not sharp enough to cut through the fabric and into Chase's actual leg and do damage.

The cop lifted his leg and studied the dangling dog for a moment, then smiled. "Aren't you just the cutest, sweetest little dog?"

I could tell that Babette wanted to respond to this, but since that meant she had to let go of her quarry, she decided to give the cop the silent treatment instead.

Unfortunately she was no match for the cop, so he simply

plucked her from his leg like one plucks an apple from a tree and held her in the palm of his hand. "And what's your name, huh?" he said. "Isn't he just the cutest, babe?"

"He is," Odelia confirmed as she tickled the doggie behind the ears.

"Now, Mr. Max!" said Babette. "They're distracted!"

Normally, I'm not all that quick off the mark, but I was feeling peckish, so I didn't need to be told twice. And while our humans enjoyed themselves with Babette, Dooley and I quickly nabbed the few remaining nuggets of kibble from her bowl. They certainly hit the spot.

"Thanks, Babette," I said.

"Don't mention it," said the doggie.

But when Odelia looked back and saw the empty bowl, her expression clouded. And I had the impression she would have said something, but at that moment, Abe walked back in, accompanied by one of his assistants, so she merely proceeded to glower at us.

Somehow, I had a feeling she wasn't happy with our work. But at least my stomach wasn't empty anymore, so we could get on with the case. I mean, it's hard to detect and hunt for clues on an empty stomach! Even detectives have to eat.

CHAPTER 4

*B*abette felt she'd done her part: she had kept her human company while she recovered from the shock of seeing that dead man on the floor, she had fed the cats and generally behaved exemplarily, if she said so herself. So she felt she deserved a break and snuck out of the house through the pet door and trotted into the modest little back-yard belonging to her family. Then, she made her way to the back fence, where she proceeded to sneak through the hole she had dug underneath, nicely obscured by a large geranium plant, and came out the other side feeling very much in her element.

Of course, it wasn't nice that people murdered each other and then left the dead bodies lying around other people's homes, but then that was humans for you: a particularly nasty breed. Except for her own humans, of course, who were just about the sweetest, nicest, most decent people around.

She glanced left and right, then stuck her nose in the air and sniffed. It took her a while to ascertain which direction she had to go, but finally, she got the scent well established in her nose, and so she trotted due east until she reached another fence, snuck underneath this one, and found herself on familiar ground. This was the backyard belonging to her good friend Fifi, whose owner wasn't as nice as hers, but then you can't always get what you want. Fifi was a Yorkshire Terrier, and Babette had been friends with her for the longest time. They enjoyed visiting each other, but also spending time at dog choir, a choir that many of the other dogs in Hampton Cove were also members of.

It was modeled after cat choir, a gathering of cats in Hampton Cove Park that was often attended by no fewer than dozens or maybe even hundreds of felines. In comparison, dog choir was a modest affair, but it was growing as its popularity spread. Dogs are, after all, sociable creatures and enjoy the company of other dogs. And as she looked around for a sign of Fifi, her eye fell on the couple that sat on the deck, enjoying a nice glass of wine and each other's company. Recently, Kurt Mayfield, as Fifi's human was called, had found love again, or so Fifi had told her, with his next-door neighbor Gilda Goldstein. And now the two were practically inseparable. Whereas Kurt had been more or less a grumpy-faced curmudgeon all his life, now he was almost human.

"The love of a good woman," Fifi had called it, though Babette found that hard to believe since her own human was a good woman, and she had loved her man intensely, and still, he had died. So apparently, the love of a good woman could do a lot, but it couldn't keep a good man from dying.

Fifi now came trotting up to her, and for a moment, they touched noses.

"Do I have a story to tell you!" said Babette. And so she proceeded to tell her friend all about the dead man who had the gall to die on their kitchen floor.

"Oh, no," said Fifi with pretty concern. "I do hope he won't linger."

"What do you mean, linger?" she asked.

"Well, you know. Dead humans have a tendency to linger. When their work on earth isn't done."

"You mean... ghosts?" she asked. When Fifi nodded seriously, she gasped in shock and horror. "Oh, no!" she said. "I don't like ghosts, Fifi."

"That's why you need to make sure your house is cleansed by a ghost hunter," said Fifi.

"A ghost hunter? What's that?"

"Ghost hunters are people who make a living hunting ghosts. They make sure all ghosts leave your premises and never return. And I think in your case, you're going to need exactly that, for these dead humans, especially the ones that have been murdered, have an inclination to stick around, feeling their life was cut off so abruptly that they simply can't believe it, and so they linger."

"But I don't want this man to linger! I don't even know him!"

"Doesn't matter. He will linger as long as his murder hasn't been solved and haunt your kitchen!"

"There were lots of detectives there," said Babette. "So one of them surely will solve this man's murder, right?"

"Who were the detectives?" asked Fifi.

"Um... I'm not sure. A man and a woman. They brought two cats along with them. One fat red one and a small sort of beige one. Though it could have been gray."

Fifi nodded knowingly. "Didn't you recognize them? They're Max and Dooley from next door."

"That's right! Max and Dooley. Max was very mean to me, and Dooley was very nice."

"Oh, but they're both super nice," said Fifi. "Max was probably playing a role. They've got this thing about interviewing suspects, you see, where they use certain techniques, and they must have figured you didn't give them what they needed, so they decided to try this technique on you. What did you tell them?"

"Nothing. I didn't have any information about the man since I'd never seen him before."

"Max will solve the case," said Fifi, who seemed to have a lot of confidence in this red cat. "But that will still leave the ghost to contend with. I'd suggest that you hire a good ghost hunter to take care of the ghost. Otherwise, you will never be at ease, Babette. That man will haunt your house forever."

Her friend's words gave her the chills. And so when Fifi finally decided that the time had come to go to dog choir, Babette's initial excitement had waned to such a degree that she thought about excusing herself and returning home. But then she thought about the police detectives and the cats and that ghost, and she decided to tag along. Dog choir would put her mind off the terrible events that had engulfed her home.

First, they passed by another friend of theirs named Rufus, and together the trio set out for the park. And as they walked along, Rufus also told her about what wonderful cats Max and Dooley were and how gifted Max was as a detective. Somehow she couldn't really see it, but then maybe this Max had to grow on her. Then again, she certainly hoped she wouldn't meet him again anytime soon.

"You have got to get that kitchen cleansed," Rufus also told her.

"But where am I going to find a ghost hunter?" she asked.

"Leave that to me," said Rufus. "I know just the right person for the job. Though I should probably say: the right cat."

Babette looked up in alarm. "A cat? Not..."

"Max," said Rufus proudly. "You can never go wrong by asking Max for his assistance. That cat is smart, Babette."

"But... I don't like Max. He's a bully."

"Max is not a bully," Rufus said. "He's kind and extremely clever. No, we have to talk to him about this ghost business. He'll be able to give us advice that will get rid of this ghost once and for all."

"O...kay," she said resignedly. Looked like she wasn't done with this red bruiser after all. Not by a long shot!

It wasn't long before they arrived at the park. If people found it strange to see three dogs roaming around unleashed and without their humans, they didn't give any indication. And so, they soon arrived at the park bench where they liked to rehearse. Dog choir didn't have an official leader or conductor like cat choir had. Mostly they simply used it as an excuse to meet other dogs and have a good time. And since Babette was feeling a little under the weather, the other dogs all decided to rally around and give her their support. Fifi had told them what happened, and they, too, all seemed to agree that Max was the cat they needed to talk to regarding this ghost business.

"Max is probably the cleverest cat that ever lived," Windex said. The Brussels Griffon had once found herself in a pickle, and Max had managed to extricate her from said pickle practically without lifting a paw. Other dogs told similar stories, like Rambo, a 200-pound retired police bulldog, and also Little John and Little Janine. This surprised Babette a great deal, as cats and dogs mostly don't get along all that well. But apparently, this Max was different. He liked all creatures and got along with all of them equally. As the stories followed, she heard how he communicated with owls and parrots and rabbits and ducks, and even with flies and ants and caterpillars and slugs!

"Odd," said Babette. "I mean, cats aren't known for their superior communication skills, are they? But this Max seems to be a different breed altogether."

"Yeah, Max is something else," Fifi confirmed. "And I think we're all very proud here to call him our friend."

It certainly was a different experience than she had had with the big red cat. Then again, maybe she should give him another chance? Once she had offered him food, he had mellowed out considerably. So maybe they had gotten off on the wrong paw? It happened. Even humans sometimes got off on the wrong foot, and then later turned into great friends. Like her own human, who by all accounts hadn't even liked her husband when they first met in high school. They had teased each other relentlessly, and everyone thought they were sworn enemies. Then all of a sudden, something must have changed, and almost overnight they had started dating and then soon after had gotten married and started a family. Too bad the guy had been killed, which had caused her human a lot of sadness, she knew.

Some kind of altercation took her out of her reverie about her family as a group of cats passed by. One of those cats was just a little bit louder than the others, and Fifi told her that this was Harriet, one of Max's friends. She was a white Persian and seemed to disagree with another female cat, this one called Shanille. The problem seemed to be about the choice of song they were going to sing that night, with Harriet insisting she perform a solo song from the oeuvre of Ed Sheeran, and Shanille saying she couldn't since Ed Sheeran was a man and Harriet was a female, and her voice wasn't a good fit.

The caravan of cats passed them by, on their way to their playground where they liked to rehearse, and Babette asked Fifi and Rufus if they always argued like this.

Fifi smiled and said that Shanille and Harriet often fought like cats and dogs, even though they were both cats, but that at the end of the day, they were great friends.

Babette found this hard to believe since they didn't look

like great friends, but then she was reminded of her small humans, Ruby and Sylvester, who also fought a lot and still seemed to love each other—in their own way. So maybe her friends were right, and it was possible to fight and still be friends.

But then it was time to start their first song of the evening, which was that perennial favorite from Elvis Presley, 'Hound Dog.' And soon they were all singing their hearts out, but no one louder than Babette.

CHAPTER 5

$\mathcal{C}$hase and Odelia had concluded their initial investigation into the death of the mystery man on Mrs. Mitchell's kitchen floor, and it was time to go home. I thought that we might still make it in time for cat choir, but unfortunately, fate decided differently. Before we left, I would have liked to say goodbye to Babette and apologize for my rude behavior, but she seemed to have vanished without a trace, possibly having stepped out into the backyard to do her business. Teacup Chihuahuas probably don't need to walk as much as their bigger canine peers and simply content themselves with a few quick laps around the backyard. But when I looked there, I saw no trace of the dog either.

Odd, I felt, and possibly alarming too. And I sincerely hoped I hadn't spooked her to such an extent that she had seen no other recourse but to escape.

"This good cat, bad cat routine may have seen better days," I told my friend as we sat on the deck and glanced around for any sign of Babette. "Obviously, I've scared the living daylights out of the poor creature."

"You weren't that bad, Max," said Dooley. "I mean, you were firm but not mean. Decisive but not harsh. Tough but not—"

"Yes, I think I get the picture, Dooley," I said.

"Clear but not... Oh, will you look at that," said Dooley, pointing to a small miniature boat that had been fashioned from Legos and placed on top of a plastic garden table. "How nice."

It *was* nice, though I reckoned it was probably a toy belonging to Holly's kids, who were of an age where they still enjoyed playing with toys. Though the ship did look extremely well done for a toy. More like something a grown-up would make, as childrens' eye-hand coordination is often not that great.

Holly now exited the house, accompanied by Chase and Odelia, presumably to talk turkey and ask her some more questions about her movements that night. But the moment Holly caught sight of the ship, she suddenly turned completely white, and Chase had to support her, or otherwise she would have fallen to the floor.

"What's wrong!" Odelia said, coming to the woman's support.

"That..." said Holly, pointing a shaking finger at the Lego boat. "That thing!"

"The Legos?" asked Chase.

She nodded, looking terrified for some reason.

Now I've seen a lot of people look at Lego pieces like these, and none of them have ever behaved quite in such a way. Mostly, they admire the craftsmanship that goes into creating these pieces, but Holly clearly did not like what she saw.

"Eric used to make them exactly like that," she said in a quaking voice.

"Eric, your husband?" asked Odelia.

She nodded. "He loved that stuff. It was his big hobby. After he died... I just got rid of everything. Sold them on eBay or gave them away to friends who had kids. I just didn't want to have anything that reminded me of him. I mean, I kept pictures, of course, and letters and such, but the Legos... I just couldn't face seeing them around every day, so I got rid of all of them."

Chase had approached the ship and put on plastic gloves. "And this wasn't here before, are you sure?"

Holly nodded. "I was out here earlier this evening, before we left for the mall, and I swear it wasn't there."

Chase had picked up the boat and turned it this way and that. Finally, he turned it over. "There's something stuck to the bottom," he announced. He proceeded to remove a small piece of paper that had been stuck to the bottom of the boat. He unfolded the piece of paper and frowned as he studied it. "Looks like a poem," he said and read, "Roses are red, violets are blue, cashews are nuts, and so are you."

We all looked up when Holly uttered a loud scream of agony.

"E-E-Eric?" she said, glancing around everywhere. "Eric?"

But of course, of Eric there was no trace. As was probably to be expected, since the man had died.

When Odelia and Chase stared at her, she pulled herself together with a supreme effort and said, "Eric used to create funny poems like that and read them to Sylvester." She suddenly burst into tears. "What's going on?"

She was right. First, a dead body in her kitchen, and now this? Who could possibly be doing this? And why?

And so the whole rigmarole started all over again: the Lego design was dusted for prints and closely scrutinized by the forensic team, and when Holly discovered that her beloved Babette had disappeared, she freaked out, and it was all Odelia could do to get her to calm down.

"They killed her," said Holly, having dissolved into tears. "The same people who murdered that poor man and put that Lego monstrosity on the table have taken Babette!"

"You don't know that," said Odelia. "Maybe she left of her own accord."

"She would never leave like that," Holly insisted. "No, she was abducted, and very soon now, they'll mail us her dead remains in a box!"

Odelia now turned to us and gave us a look that wasn't open to interpretation or discussion. We had to find Babette, and we had to find her now!

And so Dooley and I, instead of going off to cat choir to have a pleasant evening, found ourselves going on a wild-goose chase, though it was probably more accurate to call it a wild-dog chase, even though in this particular case the dog wasn't wild at all but domesticated. And since in my humble opinion only another dog can quickly find a dog, I thought it was probably a good idea to enlist the services of our canine friends, Fifi and Rufus. If anyone could find this missing Babette, it was them.

As luck would have it, the street where Holly lived was only one street over from the one where our friends lived. And so we traversed the backyard, which smelled very powerfully of Babette's particular aroma, which wasn't hard to understand since she lived there, and soon we discovered a hole that was dug underneath the fence. It was unfortunately too small for me to pass through, though Dooley had no problem. And so I had to jump that fence, which proved a challenge, and then jump down again on the other side. Now that posed an even bigger problem. Which is why I soon found myself stuck on top of that fence, seeing no way to get down again!

And so I did the only thing a cat in trouble knows how to do: I burst into loud caterwauling!

Lucky for me, Kurt Mayfield must have heard me. Unlucky for me, Kurt doesn't like it when cats caterwaul in his immediate vicinity. The man used to be a music teacher, you see, so he has very sensitive ears. So when he came stomping over and grabbed me, it wasn't with the gentle caress and sweet tenderness I would have liked to see but rather with a firm hand and a lot of cursing. The end result was the same, though: I found myself on terra firma once again, and not a moment too soon!

Unfortunately for us, we didn't find Fifi where she should have been.

Fortunately for us, we knew exactly where she might be: dog choir!

We might not make it to cat choir, but at least we'd have dog choir.

CHAPTER 6

e found Fifi in the park as anticipated, and, as luck would have it, we found her in the presence of Babette herself. The teacup Chihuahua didn't seem overly pleased to see me, so I felt I had some more apologizing and groveling to do. But before I could launch into my heartfelt apology, she trotted up to me and said, "Mr. Max, I would like to engage your services as a private investigator. I can't pay you in cash, but I can pay you in kibble. So what do you say?" She gave me a sort of trepidatious look, fully expecting me to turn her down, but I have to say I was gratified that'd gone from seeing me as some kind of ogre to wanting me to go to bat for her in my capacity as a feline sleuth.

"I'd be happy to take your case," I said, therefore. "And you can forget about the kibble. I'll do it pro bono." I felt I had some making up to do and had already told myself never to unleash my 'Mad Max' persona ever again. Clearly, it wasn't exactly my forte, since I do have a tendency to overdo things.

"But I haven't even told you what the case is yet," said Babette, much surprised by my ready agreement.

"Oh, that's fine. I shouldn't have barked at you the way I did, so consider this my atonement."

Dooley laughed. "Max, a cat can't bark. That's for dogs!"

"I know, but I still feel as if I barked at Babette."

My friend now lowered his voice. "If I were you, I wouldn't go all bonobo on her, though, Max. Bonobos are known to turn violent when confronted with other bonobos. I saw a documentary about them once, and even though they're mostly a peaceable species, it's not all sunshine and roses."

I smiled. "I said pro bono, Dooley, not bonobo."

He stared at me. "Oh, but I'm also pro bonobo, Max. I think we should protect the species at all costs, but we're not in the Congo here, you know."

I decided to let the matter rest for the moment and turned back to Babette. "So what is this case you would like me to handle?"

"I want you to get rid of this ghost, Max," she said, not exactly making her meaning fully clear.

"What ghost would that be?" I asked, therefore.

"Well, the ghost of that dead man in the kitchen, of course. Fifi told me that dead humans have a tendency to linger and provide the home with an unpleasant atmosphere, at least until their murder has been solved. So I would like you to solve that man's murder so he can move to that great realm in heaven—or hell, if he so chooses, of course."

I thought for a moment. "I was already going to try and be instrumental in solving the man's murder, Babette, since my humans have asked me to. But now I'll do my extra best. Though I have to tell you that I don't really believe in ghosts, you know."

"You don't?" asked Babette.

"Well, no. At least I've never seen any conclusive evidence that ghosts exist, so…"

Fifi had now also joined us, and Rufus as well, and clearly they were of a different mind on the whole ghost debate. "I think that ghosts do exist, Max," said Fifi. "And what's more, they can seriously mess with the living if left to their own devices. So I would strongly advise you to get on board with the pro-ghost coalition and make sure that this ghost never haunts Babette's doorstep again."

"I think the correct expression is 'darken her doorstep,'" Rufus supplied helpfully.

"Whatever," said Fifi with an irritable wave of her paw. "As long as my meaning is clear: Max should put his best paw forward to catch this man's killer so he can move on—both of them: the killer to a maximum-security penal facility and the killed on to greener pastures."

"Do you think heaven has nice pastures?" asked Dooley, interested.

"Heaven has it all, Dooley," said Fifi. "It has all the food you want, and friends to play with and shoot the breeze with, and the best bones you can find."

Dooley made a face. "I'm not so much into bones, Fifi."

"Oh, that's right," said the Yorkie. "I forgot for a moment there that you're a cat, not a dog. Well, what do cats like more than anything?"

"To take naps?" Dooley suggested.

"Okay, then heaven is the place where you can take the best naps."

"Ooh, I like that," said Dooley. "Where is this heaven that you mention?"

"It's the great beyond, Dooley," Rufus explained. "Where cats go when they've eaten their last kibble and enjoyed their last nap on earth, they move on to that great place in the sky."

Dooley glanced up at the night sky, clearly wondering

where this wonderful place might be located. But since I felt the conversation was veering off-topic, I decided to return to the matter at hand. "So this man in your kitchen, do you think he's really Eric? Your human's husband who died?"

Babette frowned. "I don't think so. Like I said, I'd never seen this man before, and I had the impression that Holly had also never seen him before. Though it's always possible that he's connected to Eric somehow. He had a lot of friends. He was a well-liked and very sociable type of person. Why?"

"Well, we found a Lego boat on the table on the deck, and your human seemed to think that it belonged to her husband. There was also a piece of paper stuck to the bottom of the ship, with a poem like the ones that Eric used to write and read to their kids. So it now looks as if—"

"It's Eric!" Fifi suddenly cried. "He's haunting your home, Babette. He's turned into a ghost and now he refuses to leave." She gave us a look of significance. "That can only mean one thing, you guys."

"What?" asked Rufus.

"That Eric was murdered! Why else would he refuse to move on?"

I felt a strong urge to roll my eyes but resisted the impulse. Instead, I argued, "According to what Holly told us, her husband was found in a ditch, where he had crashed his car after it veered off the road. The police concluded that his death was a tragic accident."

"And I say he was murdered, and they should reopen the investigation."

"I do remember how fond Eric was of his Legos," Babette now admitted. "He was a big fan and collected those big pieces and created them in the basement, which he called his man cave, for reasons I never understood. I mean, it wasn't a cave as much as a cozy and comfortably decorated basement. And Sylvester was down there all the time, and so was Holly, so it wasn't so much a man cave as a family cave, and not a cave but a basement, so he probably should have called it his family basement."

"Men like to think they're still a little wild," Fifi explained. "It's the age-old instinct. Deep down they think they're still cavemen, and so they need a cave to act out their caveman instincts."

"But Eric wasn't a caveman, though," said Babette. "He was a sales rep, representing a hygiene products company."

"Okay, so he was a clean caveman," Fifi said. "But the fact remains that he was murdered and has returned to haunt the house until his murderer is caught." She eyed me intently. "Looks like you've got two murders to solve, Max."

"And two ghosts to appease," Rufus added.

Babette gave me a look of uncertainty. "So will you need to double your usual fees, Max?"

"Yeah, two bonobos instead of one," Fifi said with a grin.

"It's fine," I said. "For one thing, I don't think Eric was murdered, but if you'd like me to, I'll definitely look into that as well. But first and foremost, we have to find out who this dead man in your kitchen is and who put him there."

Babette gave me a tentative smile. "You know, when we first met, I thought you were a bully, Max. But maybe you're not so bad after all."

"Yeah, Max," Fifi said with a wink. "Maybe you're not so bad."

"Okay, fine," I said. "So I overdid it with the good cat, bad cat stuff, and I promise I'll never do it again. But you have to admit, Babette, that you were very reluctant to answer any of our questions, so I had to do something to get you to talk."

"All you had to do was ask, Max," she said. "And I would have told you what I know, which is nothing. But you had to start bullying me into submission, and immediately that put my hackles up."

"I'm sorry," I said sincerely. "As I said, I'll never do it again."

She smiled. "It's fine. I was simply teasing you, Max. It wasn't that bad. And you're absolutely right. If you hadn't become a little forceful, I probably wouldn't have told you anything. So maybe you did the right thing."

I breathed a sigh of relief. And since cat choir was about to start, I decided to celebrate my newfound exoneration by this sweet and kind Chihuahua by joining my friends and singing my heart out. After all, as things stood, tomorrow I had to get cracking on solving not one but two cases, as well as expelling a ghost!

Now that was the kind of case I'd never cracked before. And all pro bonobo.

CHAPTER 7

*S*ince Holly felt she couldn't be in the same house where that man had died, and after being spooked to within an inch of her life by that Lego ship on her deck, she asked her mom if she couldn't stay with them for the time being. Mom happily said yes, glad that one of those empty rooms in that big house of theirs would be filled again, and so after she had told the police detective and he said he thought it was the perfect solution, she took the kids, packed an overnight bag, and off they went.

They still hadn't found Babette, but Odelia Kingsley had assured her she would be found, and somehow she believed the woman. She seemed to know what she was doing.

It was way past the kids' bedtime at this point, and they fell asleep on the short drive over. The poor dears were exhausted, and even though she had tried to keep the news about the man being found in their kitchen from them, it was obvious that they had picked something up from the conversations that had gone on around them. Before he nodded off, Sylvester had asked why a man would come to die in their house, a man they didn't even know. She'd told him that he probably wanted to take a little nap but then didn't wake up again.

Sylvester had nodded wisely, wrinkled up his nose, and said, "We should let him sleep, Mom. If he's that tired, we should just let him rest for as long as he wants to."

She and her dad carried the kids up to her old room while she took her sister Mimi's room, and before long, they were all settled in. She returned downstairs to sit in the kitchen with her parents, and together they discussed the recent events for way longer than they should have.

Dad had his own ideas about the case. "The man was probably a thief who decided that breaking into your house was a good idea. But then, for some reason, he died of a heart attack. Bad luck for him and good luck for you, or otherwise he would probably have robbed you blind."

"He didn't die of a heart attack, Dad," she said. "He was shot."

"So he had an accomplice, and they fell out. It happens all the time. Thieves falling out is so common they even made an expression out of it."

"So how do you explain the Lego boat on my garden table?"

"The thief took it! He must have found where you had hidden it and decided he could maybe sell it on eBay, but then he ended up getting into an argument with his colleague, and one shot the other, and the killer forgot to take the Lego and left it on your table. Look, it's all very simple, and I'm sure the police will clear it up in no time."

"I don't think it's that easy, Dad," she said. "For one thing, I got rid of all of Eric's Legos a long time ago. So if this guy was a thief, he couldn't have found it since there was nothing to find. And also, I've never heard of a pair of thieves breaking into a house when the owners can arrive home any moment."

"Oh, but I have," said her dad, stubborn to the last. "Only last month, a thief broke into the home of a policeman, if you please! The guy was downstairs watching television while the thief went about his business upstairs, robbing the guy blind. And the worst part is that he only found out what happened after the thief was long gone, and so were all his comic books. The guy was one of those collectors of valuable old comics. His entire collection, stolen, right from under his nose. And the guy is a cop!"

"There isn't a lot to steal at Holly's place," Mom now interjected. She had made them all tea and now placed the cups on the kitchen table and took a seat. "So if this really was a thief, he chose the wrong house."

"I never said these were clever thieves," said Dad. "If they were, they obviously wouldn't have selected Holly's house as a target."

She thought her dad actually looked pretty good, in spite of the fact that Mom claimed he was suffering from heart trouble. His face was florid, and he looked in excellent fettle. Maybe he was right, and they shouldn't move out of the big house and into a much smaller apartment. Dad had even suggested they could take in paying lodgers since they had all that space and they should put it to use.

"The police will figure it out," said Mom. "And we'll know who the dead man was and who put him in your kitchen, and this nightmare will be over. But until then, I want you to make yourself at home here, honey."

"This is her home," Dad said. "So you can stay for as long as you like."

They both gave her welcoming smiles, and she suddenly experienced a wave of emotion as she felt grateful to her folks for taking her and the kids in like this. And frankly, she didn't think she would be ready to move back to her own house for a little while. Even if they cleared up this business with the dead man, that still didn't explain how that Lego boat had gotten on her table, especially with Eric's poem stuck to the bottom.

Or could her dad be right, and did she still have parts of her late husband's Lego collection hidden somewhere? She thought she had gotten rid of the whole lot, but was it possible that maybe she had missed some?

It would certainly do a lot to alleviate her anxiety over Eric returning to his home to haunt it as a ghost. Very silly, she knew, since ghosts obviously didn't exist, and there probably was a perfectly logical explanation. But until those detectives told her exactly what happened, she didn't want to set one foot in that house again.

"So what are you going to do about your presentation?" asked Mom as she took a sip from her chamomile tea.

"I already called my boss to tell him I won't be able to go," she said. Under the circumstances, it wasn't possible to leave her kids behind to go traveling to do some presentation. "He understood when I explained what happened."

"I think that's a very wise decision," said Mom, looking very pleased that her daughter wouldn't be going on that trip. "Very, very wise." She took her daughter's hand and gave it a comforting squeeze. "I'm glad you're here, honey."

She returned her mom's smile. "I'm also glad," she said and meant it too.

CHAPTER 8

*C*at choir concluded, and we were on our way home when we came across a peculiar sight: sleeping on one of the benches placed in the park for the enjoyment of its visitors, a man lay sleeping. And when we looked a little closer, we saw that a second man lay on a second bench, and a third, and a fourth, and so on and so forth. All in all, we could see no less than seven men lying on as many benches, sleeping rough, as the vernacular goes. They didn't look all that well-groomed, quite the contrary, in fact. Dressed in clothes that had seen better days, unwashed and unshaven, it wasn't too much to say that these men represented what is often called the homeless section of society.

"I didn't know sleeping in the open air was the new trend, Max," said Dooley as he eyed the scene with interest.

"It's not a new trend," said Brutus. "It's that these people can't find a place to live apart from the park."

"But why, Brutus?" asked Dooley. "Can't they rent something? A nice apartment in town, maybe? Or a house, like we do?"

"Apartments are expensive, Dooley," said our friend. "And so are houses. Not everyone can afford to pay for them."

And as we traversed the sad scene, it became evident that there were more. The lucky ones had decided to occupy a bench, but there were others who were simply sleeping on the ground or in a sort of tent that they had constructed themselves, or even a large cardboard box.

"I find it very odd," said Harriet, "that no one would take care of them. I mean, there must be people who have plenty of space in their homes, right? Take those very large beach-front mansions, for instance. I'll bet they've got lots and lots of space that they don't need, so why not give some of it to these poor folk?"

"Not everyone likes to share their home with strangers, Harriet," I said. "Most people are not all that fond of giving up their privacy to take care of others who are perhaps in greater need than they are themselves."

"I think it's just plain selfish," said Harriet, getting a little worked up now. "I mean, it's not as if they can't afford to share, is it?"

As we walked along, I saw that at least some good Samaritans had decided to assist these unfortunate people by handing out flyers. But when I happened to glance down at one of those flyers, I saw that maybe these weren't good Samaritans after all. The message on the flyers was clear: 'Get out of Hampton Cove because you don't belong here.' And when I looked at one of those volunteers, I thought I'd seen him somewhere before. I could be mistaken, of course. Humans all look the same, after all, so it's not hard to confuse one with the other. This particular human was accompanied by a dog, and when I addressed the dog, it looked down its nose at me.

"I'm sorry," said the dog. "But I don't talk to cats, especially not cats that belong to vagrants like those people over there."

"Oh, but we don't belong to these people," I said. "We're just passing through on our way home. Say, have we met before?"

"I don't think so," said the dog, its nose still in the air. "If we had, I would remember."

I didn't know whether that was meant as a compliment or not, but somehow I had the impression it wasn't.

"What's your name?" I asked, still trying the friendly approach.

"None of your business," said the dog, who was of the poodle inclination.

For some reason, I felt a sort of anger bubbling up inside me. And before I knew what was going on, I suddenly lashed out. "Don't talk to me like that!" I yelled at the poodle. "I'm a cat, and I deserve just as much respect as you do, is that clear? Now I asked you what your name is, and if you won't tell me, I'm prepared to kick you all the way to kingdom come! Cause this is my park, and you're trespassing!"

The dog seemed taken aback by this outburst of mine, for it suddenly adopted a different, meeker tone. "Of course, of course," it said appeasingly. "My name is Melvin, and this is my human, Mark Cooper. We're simply going for a walk, that's all. No need to get your panties in a twist."

"I don't wear panties," I said, still fuming a little.

"And besides, this park doesn't belong to you," the dog continued. "It's a community park, so it belongs to all of us tax-paying citizens."

"Understood," I grunted. I must say I felt a little bit embarrassed by my outburst, the second already that day. First, I'd lost my temper to some extent with Babette, though that was entirely stage play, of course, and now with this poodle. What was going on with me? I wasn't sure, but I didn't think I liked it. Almost as if I was Bruce Banner and my inner Hulk was trying to burst onto the scene.

"So what's going on with all these people?" asked the dog.

"No idea," I said, having calmed down considerably. "They weren't here before, you know. And we're at the park every day, so we would have seen them if they were."

Dooley, Harriet, and Brutus, who had been eyeing me a little strangely after my outburst, now approached to join the conversation.

"I think they're all homeless people," Harriet said.

"Which is funny since there are probably plenty of homes they could use," Dooley added his two cents.

"So what's all this with the flyers?" asked Brutus, referring to the flyers Melvin's human was handing out.

"Oh, that," said the poodle. "Mark isn't too fond of people sleeping in the park, or on the street, for that matter. He would like to see them all go back to where they came from, wherever that is, and for the streets and the parks to return to the way they were before: full of nice people who are friends and neighbors, but not these homeless folks." He lowered his voice. "Between you and me, I think Mark isn't very fond of them for some reason. Though it is true that they take up a lot of space."

We glanced around and saw that all of the park benches had been taken, so maybe Mark Cooper had a point. "They do take up a lot of space," Harriet admitted. "Though most probably because they don't have anywhere else to go."

"Not our problem," said Melvin, some of the old belligerence returning. But he only had to take one look at me, and he quickly piped down again. "I mean, it's terrible for them, of course, but what can we do about it?"

"We could open our homes to invite these people in," Harriet suggested. "If every family in Hampton Cove adopted one of these people, they wouldn't have to sleep rough anymore. Everybody would have a place to stay, and we all would live happily ever after." One of the homeless people had woken up and now grabbed the flyer Mark had deposited on his chest. He read it, then crumpled it up and dropped it to the ground. Moments later, he was doing something with a lighter and a spoon and a needle that didn't look very healthy, in my personal opinion.

"What is he doing, Max?" asked Dooley.

"Um..."

"It looks like he's taking drugs," said Melvin.

"Or he could be a diabetic," Harriet suggested.

Somehow, it didn't strike me as very likely that this man would be diabetic, and the stuff he was injecting himself with didn't look like his medication either. More like the kind of drugs addicts like to indulge in.

A second homeless person now came walking up to us, though walking was perhaps not the right word for the activity he was engaged in. More like shuffling along like a zombie. And then it hit me. These people, they were all drug addicts!

"I think Hampton Cove Park has just become a drug clinic," Brutus said, having come to the same conclusion.

"Oh, that's right," said Melvin. "That's another reason Mark isn't happy with these people. He says they all take drugs and deposit their needles all over, creating a serious risk for the kids that play here during the day."

"Or the cats that sing here during the night," Dooley added.

It certainly presented a safety risk, I thought. If a child picked up one of these needles, there was no telling what it could do with it. Certainly nothing good could come of it.

"Maybe this isn't a matter for your human," I told the dog, "but for the police."

"Oh, but Mark has notified the police many times, and

they don't seem all that eager to remedy the situation. So he and some of our other neighbors have decided to take matters into their own hands and have formed a neighborhood watch."

We all shared a look. "A neighborhood watch?" I asked.

"Yes, that's right. Have you heard about that?"

"Oh, we have heard all about neighborhood watches," Brutus assured the poodle. "In fact, we're all part of a watch ourselves. It's run by our humans, and they patrol the streets looking for trouble."

"Not looking for trouble," I corrected him, "but looking to stop trouble."

He gave me a keen look. "With Gran in charge, trouble mostly comes looking for us."

Which was a frank assessment of the kind of neighborhood watch Gran was running, of course. Then again, her track record wasn't all bad. In the course of her checkered career as the leader of the neighborhood watch, she had caught some wrongdoers from time to time. Or she had become the wrongdoer, and the police had caught her.

Mark Cooper had finished doling out flyers, though I really couldn't see these vagrants or drug addicts heeding his admonition to take their leave. At least none of them paid the old man any attention. Melvin watched it all with a sad look in his eye.

"He tries hard, you know," he said. "But unfortunately, nobody will listen."

"Is he in charge of your neighborhood watch?" I asked.

"No, that's another person named Christopher Goldsworthy," said Melvin.

"And do you cover all of Hampton Cove?" If that was the case, this new neighborhood watch might clash at some point with Gran's neighborhood watch.

"No, we mainly patrol our own block," said Melvin, who

had become very garrulous by now, contrary to his initial position regarding talking to cats. I guess my 'bad cat' routine, even though I had promised myself not to utilize it anymore, was proving useful under certain circumstances.

"And what block would this be?" I asked.

"Russell Street and the surrounding area," said the poodle.

We all stared at the poodle in amazement. "You mean... where the dead man was found earlier tonight?" I asked.

Now it was Melvin's turn to stare at us. "How do you know about that?" he asked.

"We were there! Our human is with the police," I explained. "Odelia Kingsley? She's a reporter and civilian consultant with the police department, and her husband Chase is a police detective. They're handling the case."

"I thought I recognized you guys from somewhere!" said Melvin. "We were standing outside, at the police cordon, watching on. So who was that man?"

"No idea," I said. "At least not yet. I'm sure it won't be long before they find out."

"They'll show his picture to all the neighbors," Brutus explained. "And chances are that someone will recognize him." He shrugged. "It's simple police procedure." And as a cop's cat, he should know. He nodded toward me. "I'm sorry we couldn't be there, Max. We had, um... other stuff to take care of."

I could readily imagine what this other stuff was, as I detected a rose petal in his hair. Harriet and Brutus mostly like to spend their time in the rose bushes at the bottom of the garden, engaged in the kind of lovey-dovey stuff that doesn't leave time for visiting crime scenes. When you're a cat in love, the world of crime doesn't feature on your radar, I guess. And even though Harriet and Brutus have been together for a little while now, the love light still burns as brightly as it did when they first met.

Mark Cooper gave Melvin's leash a goodish yank, and the doggie said goodbye and expressed a wish to meet us again so we could supply him with more information regarding the strange case of the dead body found in his neighbor's kitchen.

We waved goodbye, and then Dooley said, "Max, you did your bad cat thing again!"

"I did, didn't I?" I said, feeling a touch of shame for once again having unleashed the hidden beast.

"I think you did great," said Harriet. "Sometimes you need to be firm, Max. And it clearly worked."

"I loved it," said Brutus. He grinned at me. "I didn't think you had it in you, Maxie baby."

"I didn't either," I confessed. "But when he treated me as if I was mud on his paw, I just got so angry, you know. And before I knew it, I was laying into him."

"With resounding effect," Brutus said admiringly.

"Now if we can please go home," said Harriet. "I feel a long beauty sleep coming on, and if I miss it, my beauty and gorgeousness just might be diminished by as much as three percent come morning."

And since we certainly didn't want to be held responsible for a diminishment of Harriet's beauty quotient, however slight, we started on our return journey.

CHAPTER 9

*A*nd it was as we were halfway there that I suddenly remembered the urgent missive Odelia had given us: find Babette. We had found Babette, all right, but for some reason, it had completely slipped my mind to impress upon her the turmoil her leaving had left her human in. And so, while my friends continued on their homeward trek, I decided to retrace my steps and find Babette—again—to tell her she had to return home post-haste.

I found the teacup Chihuahua where we had left her: still singing her heart out as part of the dog choir lineup. Apparently, dogs have more stamina than cats, for cat choir had finished a long time ago.

When Babette saw me approach, for a moment she seemed unsure how to respond. But when I told her that no, I hadn't found her ghost yet, and yes, I was still very much committed to taking on her case, she relaxed.

"The thing is, Babette," I told her, "that it completely slipped my mind that your human is very worried about your disappearance."

"I didn't disappear," Babette said. "I decided to go on a

mission. My mission brought me to Fifi, and then to the dog choir, and then to you. So I'd say mission accomplished and a job well done."

"The job certainly is well done," I agreed, "but the fact remains that your human is very worried about you. She thinks you may have been kidnapped or murdered, or both."

Babette's face was a nice display of emotions, which ranged from shock to dismay to guilt. "Oh, my God," she said. "I didn't think about that." She turned to her friends. "Fifi, Rufus, it's important that I return immediately. My human is very worried about me and thinks I may have been killed!"

"Oh, that happens to me all the time," Rufus assured her. "Every time I go to dog choir, in fact. Ted freaks out and thinks I've escaped or have been kidnapped, and then when I come back, he says he's going to lock me up in the doghouse from now on, and then he forgets about it again until next time."

"Wouldn't it be easier if Max told Odelia that we're going to dog choir?" said Fifi. "And then she can tell our humans? That way, they don't have to worry so much anymore."

"It would," I agreed. "But since they don't know that Odelia can talk to me, I don't think that's such a good idea."

"Yeah, there's that," Fifi admitted. "Well, anyway, I think it's time we all got back. Otherwise, all of our humans will probably think we've been murdered."

And so we all set about returning to the old homestead. And since Babette's home is right around the corner from our own, we all headed in the same direction. I don't usually travel with a pack of dogs, and so at first it felt a little unusual to me to be walking along the street in the company of no less than three canines. But since Fifi and Rufus are both old friends, and Babette was quickly turning into a new friend, it didn't take long before I relaxed and started feeling at ease.

"So what leads are you going to follow, Max?" asked Babette. "How are you going to handle this investigation into the ghost?"

"I'm not sure," I confessed. "Mostly I simply follow my instincts, you know. My intuition? Oftentimes it guides me in the right direction."

"I don't know how you do it," said Rufus with a shake of the head. "I mean, I'm a dog, so following trails and traces is second nature to me, but for the life of me, I wouldn't know where to begin."

"Well, Odelia does most of the legwork," I explained, "so I don't have to do it. She interviews suspects and witnesses and follows up on clues and such. And then Chase is a cop, so he can do background checks and look at phone records and bank records and check email and internet search history and all of that stuff. And when all is said and done, and they've collected and collated all of this data, it kinda percolates in my head for a while, and usually, something comes out the other end."

"Like a sausage factory," Fifi said knowingly. "You put a lot of meat in at one end, and then at the other end of the production line, a nice sausage comes out."

"Mmm, sausage," said Rufus, and I think he was hungry, for his eyes drooped closed for a moment even as his tongue dangled from his lips.

"Yeah, more or less," I agreed. "You put in a lot of information on one end, and then on the other end, a conclusion comes out. It's not hard once you get the hang of it. The only problem is that you need to find that one moment of inspiration, and that's often hard to come by. I know it often takes me a lot of agonizing over the case before I hit on the one thing that will spark an idea."

"It certainly is inspiring for me," Babette confessed.

"It is inspiring, isn't it?" said Fifi. "To take a peek behind the curtain and see how the mind of a great detective works?"

I gave her a look of mild embarrassment. "I'm not really much of a detective, you guys," I said. "Just trying to give a helping paw to my human, you know."

"Just like I like to lend a helping paw to my human," said Babette, nodding approvingly. We had arrived at her house, though when we glanced up at it, there were no lights on, which meant that her humans must have retired to bed, and my humans must have left. We accompanied our new friend around the back and watched her go in through the pet door. And we were just about to proceed to our own homes when she came storming out again.

"They're gone!" she cried, looking distinctly dismayed. "All of them are gone!"

"What do you mean, gone?" asked Fifi.

"They're not there! The house is empty." She placed a paw to her face. "Oh no! They've been kidnapped, Max! Taken! Or even..." She gulped once or twice. "Killed!"

"I don't think they would be kidnapped," I assured her, thinking fast. And then I had it. "Probably they decided they couldn't stay here because of the murder, so they're staying with a friend, perhaps? A family member?"

Relief flooded Babette, and her face relaxed. "Of course. They're probably staying with Holly's mom and dad."

"Do they live far from here?"

"No, just around the corner." She heaved a sigh of relief, then scrunched up her face. "Would you mind terribly... I mean, if it's not an imposition, could you possibly..."

"Accompany you?" asked Fifi. "Of course. It will be our pleasure."

And so we set out to take Babette home—her second

home, apparently. After the shock she'd had, it was only to be expected that she wouldn't like to walk along those deserted streets of our neighborhood all alone. Before long, we had rounded the corner, and oddly enough, we were met by a car that stood parked along the street, its headlights blinking at us for some reason.

Though, of course, they could simply be blinking in general, not specifically at anyone in particular.

A man now came hurrying up and got into the car's backseat. Then all was quiet again.

"Don't mind them," Babette said, paying scant attention to the strange and frankly disturbing scene. "They're members of the neighborhood watch. They like to patrol the streets at night, allegedly to keep us all safe. But considering a dead body was found in our kitchen, it's obvious they're not doing a very good job."

She had a point, of course, since it's probably the purpose of a neighborhood watch to watch out for exactly this type of nefarious activity.

We passed the car, and when I glanced up, I saw a man looking down at me. He was handsome to a degree and wouldn't have looked out of place on a poster for a Hollywood movie.

"Who is that?" I asked, curiosity getting the better of me.

"Christopher Goldsworthy," said Babette. "He runs the neighborhood watch."

"Oh, I remember," I said. "We met a dog at the park earlier. His name was Melvin, and he told us all about the watch."

"Yeah, I know Melvin," said Babette. "He's nice. His human? Not so much."

"His human was handing out flyers to induce the homeless people in the park to skedaddle," I said. "Though I didn't think he got a lot of applause from them. Mostly they seemed to ignore him."

"Most people on the block ignore the watch," Babette said. "I know that Holly does. They're just a bunch of annoying curmudgeons who like to meet up to complain about things. According to them, the world is going to hell in a handbasket, and if they don't act now, things will fall apart, society will perish, and yadda yadda. Holly told them from the beginning that she didn't want to have anything to do with them, and even though they weren't happy about it, they have left us in peace. Mostly."

"What do you mean, mostly?"

"Well, you know, they more or less overlap with the WhatsApp group for the dog owners in our neighborhood. So every time Holly takes me for a walk and meets with the others, all they seem to be able to talk about is watch business. So much so that Holly has taken to walking me all by herself, avoiding these people like the plague. But since they're everywhere, they're very hard to avoid."

"Oh, dear," I said.

We had arrived at the house where her human's parents lived, and this time we struck gold: there was a light on in a downstairs room, and when we trotted up to the door, and Babette let out a loud bark, moments later the door opened, and Holly appeared.

To say that the reunion of human and canine was touching would be an understatement. Even I was touched to a degree, and not a few tears were shed all around.

And since my own beauty sleep was in urgent need of a touch-up, we all decided to go home and relax in our baskets —for the dogs—or the whole house—for me. Tomorrow was another day, hopefully filled with exciting new clues and promising leads.

CHAPTER 10

he sun broke bright and early, invading the bedroom with its annoying habit of caressing my eyelids until I saw no other recourse than to drape my paw over them in a bid to hang on to those last vestiges of lingering slumber. Odelia must have experienced the same phenomenon, if her soft groans were any indication. Chase, of course, was the first one to rise, but then he's always been the athletic type. He's the kind of person who will be fast asleep one moment and jumping out of bed, ready for the new day the next. I have no tolerance for his kind, to be honest. Contrary to most cats, I need a little while to adjust to the state of full wakefulness, and even then I would much prefer if that sun would pop back down below the horizon and give us another half hour—or three.

But then I guess the sun doesn't come with a snooze option: once it pops up, it doesn't pop down again, at least not until later in the day.

"Max," said Dooley, stretching. "Have you discovered who killed that poor man yet?"

"Dooley, I have literally only been sleeping for the past

couple of hours, so how could I possibly have solved this murder already?"

"Oh, I don't know. Sometimes it seems to me as if inspiration simply strikes you out of the blue, so now I thought maybe it had struck you in the middle of the night."

"Well, it hasn't, and as long as we don't even know who this man is, I don't think there will be a lot in the form of any inspiration striking, whether at night or during the daytime." I yawned cavernously.

"Is it just me, or do you still sound like that bad cat you were doing so well last night?"

I stared at my friend. "Do you think so?"

He shrugged. "Could be just me, Max, but you sound irate." And when I didn't immediately respond, he explained, "That means cranky."

"I know what irate means, Dooley," I said, perhaps a little irately, I belatedly realized. And maybe he was right. Maybe I was irate. Though I couldn't have told you why that might be so. Perhaps I had gotten up on the wrong side of the bed? But that couldn't be it, since I hadn't gotten up at all. Not yet. And the side of the bed I was lying on was my usual side: Odelia's side. And it hadn't caused me any irritation before. It was all very odd. And since I certainly didn't want this moody mood to linger, I took great pains to hop down from the foot of the bed and avoid any sides whatsoever.

I traipsed down to the kitchen, where Chase was already busy preparing breakfast while Odelia was still wondering whether she should get up or not, and as I tucked into a few nuggets of kibble, I wondered once again if this bad cat routine I'd adopted last night was perhaps indicative of a deeper sentiment I'd been struggling with. After all, when you associate with crime and mayhem for too long, maybe some of that rubs off on you?

I'd just read that a well-known psychologist had

warned that listening to true crime podcasts and reading true crime books might indicate underlying psychological issues, and I now wondered whether that was what was going on with me. Maybe I should focus on something more wholesome from now on instead of immersing myself in these criminal cases and hobnobbing with hardened elements of the underworld. Maybe watch a Hallmark movie? Or nature documentaries, like Dooley?

The pet door gently flapped in the breeze, and Harriet and Brutus walked in. Harriet looked radiant, and clearly her beauty sleep had done her a world of good. "I just had a brilliant idea, Max," she announced.

"What is it?" I asked, hopping up on the couch to give myself up to contemplation of the brighter side of life—the non-criminal side.

"Well, so both Holly Mitchell and her poodle—"

"Teacup Chihuahua," I corrected her.

"—are convinced that their home is haunted, right?"

"Yes, both by her deceased husband and by this person found dead last night."

"Well, why don't we spend the night in their home and ascertain once and for all whether what they're saying is true?" She gave me a triumphant look. "Max, we're going to be ghost hunters!"

Oh, dear. "Look, ghosts don't exist," I told her. "We all know that."

"True, but Holly doesn't know that. She believes that ghosts exist. And we're going to prove conclusively that she's wrong. That whoever put that Lego ship on her deck wasn't a ghost but a real human person."

"Why would anyone do that?" asked Brutus. "I mean, it's very mean, isn't it?"

"It is mean," I agreed.

"I don't know," said Harriet. "To send her a message, maybe, something to do with her dead husband?"

"It's possible," I said. "But what message?"

"Well, maybe Holly's husband didn't die an accidental death. Maybe he was murdered—by her! And now someone has found out and wants her to know that they know."

"The police investigation concluded that Eric Mitchell's death was accidental," I pointed out.

"Okay, so we all know that these police investigations can be flawed," said Harriet. "So what if they were wrong, and Holly did something she shouldn't have? Or maybe someone else murdered her husband for reasons that we don't know yet, and now they're coming after his wife!"

"Look, this is all a lot of speculation," I said. "Let's just stick to the facts, shall we? All we know right now is that a dead man was found in Holly Mitchell's house last night, and so first we need to ascertain who this man is, why he was murdered, and by whom. Then we can proceed from there."

"Fair enough," Harriet agreed. And since there didn't seem to be a lot more to be said on the subject, both she and Brutus approached Chase, who had been baking an omelet, with a view of persuading the cop to let them partake in his breakfast. Yes, cats do like eggs from time to time!

Odelia now joined us, carrying Grace in her arms, the two of them yawning up a storm, causing the rest of us to join her.

"Oh, Max," said Odelia. "Did you find Babette?"

"Yes, I did," I said proudly. "And she's already been reunited with her human."

"You shouldn't have tucked into her food last night," she said. I gave her a shamefaced look. Frankly, I had hoped she would have forgotten all about that already, but obviously she hadn't.

"I'm sorry," I said. "I thought it would be fine, since Babette gave us permission."

"I know she did, but still."

"She also told us a lot of very interesting stuff that might have a bearing on your investigation."

"Well, spill," said our human as she took a seat at the kitchen counter, prepared to let herself be served by her husband.

And so I told her all about the neighborhood watch, Christopher Goldsworthy sitting in his car, Mark Cooper handing out flyers in the park, and Babette's wish for us to conduct an investigation into the presence of ghosts in her house.

"Those homeless people are a problem," Odelia mused as she gratefully accepted a piece of toast and buttered it. "They've suddenly descended on our town out of nowhere, and they refuse to budge. Many of them are drug users, apparently, and generally it's becoming a serious problem."

"Alec says he has no idea how to deal with the issue," Chase chimed in. "He's holding a meeting with Charlene today, and hopefully, they'll find a solution. People are complaining, and rightly so. These people see no qualms in using drugs right out in the open, in front of everyone, kids included. It's not a good thing for Hampton Cove, babe."

"I know," said Odelia. "But what can we do? Apart from encouraging them to admit themselves to a drug rehabilitation program or to be taken to a homeless shelter."

Chase nodded. "That's what Alec is going to discuss with the Mayor today. They're thinking about setting up a major program in town. But what's so odd is that we never had this problem before. All of a sudden, they all started showing up here."

"Other cities have been faced with the same problem. I guess now it's our turn."

"So what are we going to investigate today?" asked Dooley.

"Well, first, we have to interview all of Holly Mitchell's neighbors," said Odelia. "Ask them if they noticed anything out of the ordinary last night or heard the sound of a gunshot."

"Where were Holly and her family when this happened?" I asked.

"Out shopping," said Odelia as she took a sip from her coffee.

Meanwhile Grace was enjoying a glass of milk. She seemed to take a keen interest in what we were discussing, for she now asked, "What is a drug addict, Max?"

We all shared a look of surprise since I didn't think it was right of us to expose her to this kind of ugliness.

"Well, it's a person who likes to use drugs," I said.

"What are drugs?" was her next and probably inevitable question.

"Um… well, drugs are substances that can induce a certain mood in a person. For instance, drugs can make you feel happy when you're sad."

"Or vice versa," Harriet added.

"Or they can make you feel self-confident when you're shy."

"Or the other way around."

"And, in general, they alter the chemical balance in the brain."

"So, is that a good thing or a bad thing?" asked Grace.

We shared another look. "Well…" I said.

"It's not a good thing," Brutus said. "You don't want random chemicals to mess with your brain, Grace. Before you know it, you will start acting funny, and people will think there's something seriously wrong with you."

"But I like to be funny," said Grace. "I like to make people laugh."

"Well, that may be so, but it's probably better to do it without the assistance of any mind-altering substances," I told her.

"So if anyone offers you drugs, just say no," said Brutus. "Is that understood?"

Grace grinned at him. "Yes, Brutus." And so she proceeded to hand the glass of milk back to her mother. "I'm just saying no, Mom!" she shouted and poured the milk all over Odelia's front!

"What did you do that for!" Odelia cried.

"Well, everyone knows that milk alters the chemical balance of the brain," Grace explained. "So milk is a drug, and Brutus just told me to say no to drugs!"

"She thinks milk is a drug," I explained to Odelia, who seemed a little surprised by her daughter's sudden initiative.

"Milk isn't a drug, honey," said Odelia, hoisting her daughter on to her lap. "Milk is good for you. So please don't pour it on me, ok?"

"I'm sorry, Mom," said Grace ruefully. "I guess I was misinformed." And since she was looking intently at Brutus when she spoke these words, it was clear where this misinformation had come from, in her opinion.

"All I said was not to take drugs," Brutus sputtered. "I never said anything about milk!"

"It's all right, sugar britches," said Harriet. "We've all been young and—"

I had the feeling she was going to add 'stupid,' but catching Grace's eye, she pulled up short and swallowed her words.

No more was said on the delicate topic, and the conversation moved onto other things. Like the fact that Grace was happy that her daycare was open for business again after

Chantal Jones had been out of commission for a little while due to an incident she had been involved in. The little girl had missed her friends and was glad to return. And I think Odelia and Chase were also glad.

The door to the kitchen now swung open, and Gran burst in.

"What's all this I hear about a body being found?" she demanded.

"Holly Mitchell's house," Odelia said as she surveyed her wet shirt and wet jeans.

"What happened to you?" asked Gran. "You look like a drowning victim."

"Milk," said Odelia curtly but refused to say more for fear of returning to a topic that she considered closed.

"I should have been there," said Gran. "I mean, the watch should have been there and caught this murderer in the act."

"Were you out patrolling again last night?" asked Chase.

"We were," Gran confirmed. "But not around here. We decided to patrol the billionaire mile for a change. Those are some mighty fine mansions."

"They are mighty fine mansions," Odelia agreed, "but they also have some mighty fine security systems, so I don't think they need the watch to keep an eye out for them, Gran."

"Oh, but we just figured we'd take a look, you know. The last couple of nights have been really quiet, so we sort of got bored and decided to expand our perimeter." She gave Chase a wink as she said it, eliciting a grin from the cop as he recognized a kindred spirit when Gran used his lingo.

"There is a second watch, you know," said Odelia. "Max just told me all about it. Apparently, it's being run by a man named Christopher Goldsworthy and involves several people who live on Russell Street."

"A second watch!" Gran cried, greatly dismayed.

"I don't think there's a law against starting your own watch," Chase pointed out.

"What is a watch, Max?" asked Grace.

"Well, it's people who like to watch... other people, so they can look out for... other people." I had the impression my explanation hadn't really ticked all of her boxes, for she stared at me, clearly mystified.

"A neighborhood watch is when a bunch of neighbors patrol their neighborhood to make sure it's safe," Brutus explained.

"So a watch is what you guys do, right?" asked Grace. "Since you like to walk around at night to see if people are behaving?"

"Something like that," I admitted. "Though Gran does it so much better. She and Scarlett drive around at night looking for crimes being committed."

"And then when they see a criminal, they run," Brutus said with a grin.

"Hey, I heard that!" Gran cried. "We don't run—we intercept! And I've got the tools to prove it!"

It was true that Gran employed all the tools of her trade to intercept crooks. She had pepper spray and even a stun gun. Though when things really got tough, she called in the cavalry, in the form of the police. As, of course, she should.

"They saw one of the members of this watch handing out flyers to the homeless people in the park last night," Odelia continued.

"I wouldn't call them homeless, dear," said Gran. "They're all addicts, every last one of them. And frankly, I have absolutely no idea how they got there. First, there were none, and then all of a sudden, they're all over the place!"

"Well, now that they're here, we have to find a way to deal with them," Chase reiterated. "And we will," he promised when Gran opened her mouth to protest. "So you don't have to concern yourself with them, Vesta."

"Oh, but I've got my own solution all lined up and ready to go," Gran announced.

Chase's face clouded. "Please tell me it isn't so."

"It is so! Scarlett and I have a plan, and it's a doozy."

"I'll bet it is," said the cop, and since he wasn't a big fan of the ordinary citizenry inserting themselves in police business, even if they were his own family, he wagged a finger in the old lady's face. "Leave those people alone, Vesta."

"I will definitely *not* leave them alone," she said with a slight smile.

It was obvious she was up to something, and she wasn't going to tell us what it was until she had already gone and done it.

I just hoped she wouldn't interfere with our investigation into the case of the mysterious dead man found last night. It's hard enough to investigate a murder, and even harder when certain old ladies start stirring up all kinds of trouble.

CHAPTER 11

As often happens at the start of a new case, Dooley and I found ourselves ensconced with Chase and Odelia in Uncle Alec's office. The Chief had received a preliminary report from the coroner on the dead man and was now reading Abe's conclusions to his rapt audience.

"Okay, so the man was killed with a twenty-two-caliber bullet to the chest. The bullet entered the heart, and death must have been instantaneous. So far, we still don't have a clue who the dead man could be, but judging from the state of the body and the clothes he was wearing, Abe says he must have been sleeping rough for a number of years. He estimates the time of death around eight o'clock last night, age of the man between forty and fifty, and no wallet, phone, or other personal items were found on the body." He looked up. "Plenty of evidence to suggest he was a drug addict. Needle marks, bad teeth, skin sores, damaged liver, stomach, kidneys, bladder… So I think it's safe to say he was probably one of the people who have been seen in the downtown area and the park lately."

"We'll go and have a chat," Chase said. "See if they recognize him."

"I think it's probably not hard to imagine that two addicts broke into Mrs. Mitchell's home last night. For some reason, they got into an altercation, one of them killed the other, and then fled the scene. So let's find out who the dead man was and take it from there. Any questions? Suggestions?"

"Max told us that there's a neighborhood watch active on Holly's street," said Odelia. "So it's probably a good idea to talk to them as well. They were patrolling the street last night, so maybe one of them saw something."

"Excellent," said the Chief. "Though this business about a neighborhood watch patrolling Russell Street is news to me. They're not officially registered, that's for sure."

"I guess anyone can patrol their street at night and call themselves a neighborhood watch," said Chase.

"That's true," said the Chief. He placed his hands flat on his desk. "Okay, if there's nothing else…"

"There's also the matter of the Legos, Uncle Alec," said Odelia.

The Chief stared at her with a blank look. "Legos?"

"Yes, we found a boat made out of Legos on Holly's deck last night. Underneath, a note had been placed. It was a funny poem that Holly's husband used to write for Sylvester when he was little. The moment she heard the poem, she burst into tears and said only her husband could have written it. She even thought Eric must have returned from the dead."

"She wasn't thinking straight when she said that," Chase pointed out.

"I know, but it's very mysterious how that boat and that note would have ended up there."

"The kids must have put it there," said the Chief. "Legos and a funny poem? How old are those kids?"

"Four and eight."

"Well, there you have it. The oldest one probably wrote the poem and left it on the table along with the boat. Mystery solved. Now if there's nothing else…"

It was clear he didn't want to entertain any crazy ghost theories about the Legos, and so we were all ushered out of his office. The theory of Sylvester leaving that note was tempting, if not for the fact that Holly had insisted that she had removed all of her husband's Legos from the house and wouldn't allow them. Plus, when his dad was killed, Sylvester was four. So would he remember the funny poems his dad used to read to him and decide to reproduce them now? It was possible, of course. Then again, it still struck me as strange and definitely something we needed to look into a little more.

We would soon get our chance since Odelia planned to pay another visit to Holly, but first, we had to brave the local community of addicts, who may or may not have been intimately familiar with our dead man. Though in all likelihood, I would have said that the chance that they were was high.

Before long, we found ourselves back on familiar stomping grounds: the park where only last night those homeless people who had been asleep on their respective benches were now teeming with life as they washed themselves in a local fountain, begged money from passersby, bummed cigarettes from dog walkers, and generally spent their time looking slightly out of it, if I had to be honest. It's also possible they were engaged in more nefarious activities, such as there were: dealing, using drugs and stealing from innocent passersby to support their habit. But of that, I couldn't be sure.

Odelia and Chase went from person to person showing them the picture the coroner had taken of the dead man, and it didn't take them long before they got a hit. Turned out the man answered to the name Antoine O'Neil and had indeed been part of this local troupe.

"Yeah, I definitely recognize him," said one of the people Chase and Odelia spoke to. This man's name was Toby Grave, and he seemed a little surprised to see a picture of his friend Antoine. "What happened to him? He looks like he's asleep or something."

"I'm sorry to have to tell you this, sir," said Odelia. "But Antoine died last night."

The man seemed taken aback by this. "He died? But how?"

"He was shot," Chase explained. "He was found trespassing in a house in town. Though when the homeowner came upon him, he had already been shot."

"I knew this was going to happen," said the man. He had a sort of crazy look in his eyes, and I could tell that he was definitely in need of a shave and a bath. Then again, maybe not. There is a certain appeal to some people of adopting what is often called the 'hobo chic' look. Celebrities will pay good money to look exactly like Toby Grave did. Others have even made it their trademark look.

"What do you mean?" asked Chase.

"He kept telling us that he was going to hit it big one of these days. So I knew he had plans of breaking into some place and getting away with a nice fat haul. Only the homeowner must have caught him and decided to shoot him instead of calling the cops."

"She claims not even to have noticed Mr. O'Neil entering her home," said Odelia.

"Of course, she noticed him. She caught him red-handed with his hands in the safe, so she decided to take the law into her own hands and shoot him on the spot. I know these people," he said, wagging a finger in Chase's face. "They think just because they're rich, they can get away with anything."

His face sagged. "And probably they're right. Who is a judge going to believe: me or this rich person?"

"I can assure you that this particular person is not rich," said Chase. "Quite the contrary, in fact."

"She's a widow with two kids," Odelia explained. "Working hard to make ends meet. So if your friend chose her as a target, he made a pretty lousy choice, Toby."

"But she shot him! She shot him in cold blood! You're having her arrested, right?" But when Odelia and Chase remained stony-faced, he threw up his hands. "I don't believe this! It's all about class justice, isn't it!" He tapped Chase's chest with a not-very-clean finger and got right up into the detective's face. "You have to arrest this woman, Chief. You have to. She's gone and murdered my friend in cold blood. You can't let her get away with that, you hear me? Otherwise, you're no better than she is!"

While Chase and Odelia were chatting with Toby, Dooley and I decided to take a closer look at the man's meager belongings. Cats are curious that way. We sniffed his stash, which seemed mainly to consist of a cardboard box, a couple of blankets and a tin pot where he presumably cooked his modest but wholesome meals. What we also found was a security blanket in the shape of a rabbit, which seemed a little odd. And when we looked closer, we saw that it featured the name 'Ruby' as its proud owner.

And since I had the distinct impression this find might prove useful to the investigation, I took it between my teeth and dragged it over to where Odelia and Chase were still trying to induce Toby to give them some background information on his good friend Antoine O'Neil.

When Odelia caught sight of the security blanket, her expression hardened. The effect on Toby was immediate. One look at the blanket, which had now been transferred to Odelia's hand, and he turned a little shifty-eyed. The next moment he had broken into a run, immediately chased by Chase.

The old gag about drugs being bad for your health was about to be firmly established, for it didn't take more than thirty yards for Chase to capture the errant vagrant and outfit the man with a pair of shiny handcuffs. Turns out drugs don't improve your cardiovascular capacity as much as one would expect.

CHAPTER 12

$\mathcal{C}$hase was ensconced with Toby Grave in the confines of interview room number two. Interview room number one was occupied by a girl who had recently lost her toy and wanted to file an official complaint against her mom and dad for purposely getting rid of it because they felt she was too old to play with toys. On the table in front of Mr. Grave lay a different toy, in the form of the security blanket that had once belonged to Holly Mitchell's daughter and had been found in the man's possession.

"This proves that you broke into Mrs. Mitchell's home," Chase was saying as he pointed to the rabbit. "Or, at the very least, were instrumental in or had knowledge of your good friend Mr. O'Neil doing the same. So you better start talking, Toby."

Toby gave the security blanket a sad look, as if it had betrayed him, which in a sense it had. "Okay, fine," he said. "So Antoine wanted to hit the place. He claimed it held untold riches, which, to be honest, I didn't agree with him on. But since he was my friend, and he wanted me to be on the lookout, I went along with it. So we first cased the joint, then when we had ascertained that no one was home, we took a look-see."

"When was this?"

"Two nights ago."

"And what did you find?"

"Nothing much, just as I'd expected. No cash, no jewelry, no nothing. And we went through that place top to bottom. In the end, the only thing I took was this security blanket, and some food from the fridge. The rest I left untouched. Especially when I saw a picture in the living room that showed the family that lived there. Mom and dad and two little kiddies. I just couldn't bear to steal from them, you know." He sighed and hung his head. "Before I ended up living on the street, I worked as a security guard and tried to support my own family. But then my wife left and took my son with her, and I got into such a funk that I ended up losing everything. Not just my family but also my job, my home, and my health. So I couldn't bring myself to steal from these people."

"And what about Antoine? What did he take?"

"Nothing much. I heard him rooting around in the attic for a while, and when he came down, he looked puzzled, as if he hadn't found what he was looking for. The only thing he took was a picture."

"A picture of Holly Mitchell's family?"

Toby nodded. "He said it reminded him of his own family. Like me, he once was a family man, but because of a personal tragedy, he ended up losing everything. I guess he didn't have the heart to rob them either. So we decided to hit a different place the next night, and this time, hopefully, come away with a bigger haul. Only the next night, Antoine was nowhere to be found. Until you showed up and told me he'd been shot."

"So he returned to the same house and was shot," said Chase in conclusion.

"Guess he should have asked me to join him so I could stand watch. The family must have arrived home, caught Antoine in the act, and shot him. Which is why they're the ones you should be looking at, not me," he said, some of the old fire returning.

"One thing that isn't clear to me," said Chase, "is why exactly Antoine decided to target this particular house. What was it about the Mitchell residence?"

"According to him, he got a tip-off that there was 'untold riches' to be found in the place, but in the end, there was nothing."

"A tip-off from who?"

Toby shrugged. "Beats me. All I know is that it was a woman."

"A woman approached Antoine and told him to rob the Mitchell place?"

"That's what he said. Though it wouldn't surprise me if he made it up. Antoine had a very fertile imagination. I guess living on the street will do that to you."

"Or taking a lot of drugs," I commented.

"It's a sad story, isn't it, Max?" said Dooley.

We had been watching along with Odelia from behind the safety of a one-way mirror while Chase grilled the man. And it was indeed a sad tale the vagrant was telling the detective. But that didn't discount the fact that he and Antoine O'Neil had broken into Holly's home to steal from her. The fact that they had gotten cold feet didn't change that. And Antoine had even decided to return a second night, possibly since he felt he hadn't found what he was looking for the first time. Money, maybe? Or other valuables? At any rate, someone had caught up with him and shot him. And if Toby was correct, this person could only have been Holly herself.

Chase finished his interview with the man and left him in the good care of one of his officers who would escort the man back to his cell, where he would await further developments.

Chase joined us and seemed puzzled. "Now why would O'Neil return to the Mitchell place a second night in a row if he didn't find what he was looking for the first time? And who is this mystery woman who tipped him off?"

"The woman could be a figment of his imagination," said Odelia. "And the stuff O'Neil and Grave were after was probably money or jewelry they could pawn. These people are drug addicts, babe. They're always looking for money to pay for their next fix. It's all they can think about. The one thing that dominates their every waking moment. He probably figured Holly must have hidden her cash somewhere, or her jewelry, and since he hadn't found it the first night, he decided to return and try his luck a second time. Only this time his luck ran out—permanently."

"What do you think about this story that Holly shot him?"

"Well, she doesn't have a firearms license. And also, her mom confirmed that the family left for the mall around six, and only returned shortly before nine, which is when Holly found the dead man."

"Yeah, if the coroner is correct, and the time of death was eight o'clock, that puts Holly in the clear."

"And puts Toby Grave firmly in the frame," said Odelia. "I think it's very likely that he did accompany his friend O'Neil for the second break-in, only this time they got into some kind of argument and Toby shot his friend point-blank with that gun."

"No gun was found in Toby's possessions," Chase pointed out. "And we talked to some more of his friends, and they all claim Toby never left the park last night."

Odelia shrugged. "I'm not sure how reliable the word of a fellow addict is. They could all be covering for each other."

"It's possible," Chase allowed, but he didn't look entirely convinced. So I had a feeling the investigation wasn't over yet. Which was probably a good thing because I had my own parallel inquiry to contend with: getting rid of the ghost that allegedly now haunted Holly Mitchell's house. I would have told Odelia about this, but I had a feeling she wouldn't put a lot of credence in this ghost business, so I decided not to bother her with it. After all, she had enough on her plate with the living. No reason to add ghosts to the mix as well.

CHAPTER 13

*a*fter our detour to the police station to put Mr. Grave under lock and key for the present, Chase drove his squad car to the home of Holly's parents, Bethany and Charlie Williams. The Williamses lived in a very nice row house that, with its exposed red-brick facade and plenty of flowers to lend color and put a smile on passersby's faces, immediately put to bed the qualms I may have had about the Mitchell family being forced out of their home after it had been turned into a crime scene.

"I just can't believe that Holly would do such a thing," Dooley now confessed. "She's such a nice person, and a mother, too."

"Even mothers can turn homicidal, Dooley," I said, though I didn't put a lot of credence in the notion that Holly would have shot the intruder. But still, when you're a detective, you can't let your personal feelings take over. And no matter how nice and kind Holly Mitchell was, or how much she had suffered after her husband had died, we still had to include her in our investigation. There was a distinct possibility that she and her mother had both lied about the hour of their return from the mall.

It was Holly herself who opened the door and escorted us into a spacious and modern kitchen that wouldn't have looked out of place in a Nancy Meyers movie. I almost expected Meryl Streep or Diane Keaton to join us. Instead, the family that gathered at the kitchen table consisted of Holly herself, her mom Bethany, and her dad Charlie. The kids were in the living room watching television, and Holly had closed the connecting door so they wouldn't overhear our conversation. She explained how she tried to shield them from the whole sordid business of the dead man as much as possible.

"Sylvester already knows something," Holly's mom pointed out. "And he'll hear the rest of the story from his friends at school. So maybe you should tell him before they do—adding a lot of stuff you don't want."

"No one will tell them, since no one will know," said Holly stubbornly.

"Oh, honey, everyone will know," her dad said. "People talk, and in this neighborhood even more than elsewhere. By this time, the story will have done the rounds, and since kids are clever, they will have picked up the story from their parents, not all of whom are as careful as you are to conceal the horrible truth from them. So chances are that their friends in school will know all about it."

"If you want, I'll talk to them," Holly's mom suggested.

Holly smiled a grateful smile. "That's all right. For now, I would like to protect them from the horrible truth as long as possible. Can you imagine having to live in a place where a dead man was found? And on our kitchen floor, no less, where we all spend a lot of time as a family. I mean, it freaks me out just thinking about it, so I can only imagine how much it will freak them out."

"I think you'll find that kids are very resilient," Odelia said. "And it's always better if you can explain things to them instead of them hearing some sensational story from their friends at school."

"Yeah, maybe you're right," Holly agreed. She sighed deeply. "So have you found out anything more about that man?"

"We know his name was Antoine O'Neil," Chase said. "And that he was a homeless person who had been living in the park for the past couple of weeks. We also know that he broke into your house the night before and stole this from you." He held up the security blanket, and Holly gasped in shock.

"He broke into the house before?"

"Yes, the night before, along with a friend of his named Toby Grave. The two of them hoped to find money or valuables, but when they didn't find anything, they left again. Only for Mr. O'Neil to return, alone or together with Mr. Grave, that part isn't clear to us yet, to take a second look."

"Probably they figured you had a safe hidden somewhere," Holly's dad grunted.

"No safe," Holly said. "Because I don't have any valuables to hide."

"So what else did they take?" asked Holly's mom.

"Nothing special," said Chase. "According to Mr. Grave's statement, he didn't take anything apart from the blanket and some food from the fridge. And his friend rummaged around in the attic for a while but then only took a picture of your family, saying it reminded him of his own family, which he lost in a personal tragedy."

"Oh, how sad," said Bethany Williams.

"How sad!" her husband cried. "These drug addicts break into your daughter's home and all you can say is 'How sad?' How about 'How awful?'"

"How did they get in?" asked Holly.

"Through the back door," said Chase. "Both times."

"I told you that lock isn't worth a thing," said her dad. "You better install an alarm now."

"I didn't notice anything missing," said Holly, who seemed even more spooked now that she knew the men had been in her home two nights in a row. "Apart from Ruby's security blanket. Though I didn't believe her when she said it had been taken. I just figured she had lost it somewhere. And I did notice all of my yogurt was gone, but I figured Mom had taken it."

"I don't even like yogurt," her mom announced. She palmed the blankie affectionately. "Can we keep this?"

"Yeah, our forensic team has checked it for evidence," said Chase, "but apart from the fact that it isn't as nice and clean as it was before, nothing of note was found on it."

"No fingerprints on a blanket," said Charlie Williams.

"They did check it for DNA, but the results will take a while to process," said Chase. "So our most likely suspect right now is behind bars. That is Mr. O'Neil's friend, Toby Grave. But since we can't prove that he was at the scene at the time of the murder, we're going to keep the investigation going and look for other possible leads. There is one thing we would like to ask. According to Mr. Grave, a woman tipped off O'Neil that there was 'untold riches' to be found in your home. Do you have any idea who this woman could be or what riches she was referring to?"

"A woman told these men to break into my home?"

Chase nodded. "Mind you, it's possible that Grave is lying, or that O'Neil made it all up. But still, it might be an interesting lead to pursue."

Holly swallowed, and it was clear that the story of the woman had rung a bell with her. So we all sat up a little straighter as she exchanged a look with her mom. The latter nodded in encouragement. "Better tell them, sweetheart."

"Tell us what?" asked Odelia.

"I... I didn't think it was relevant," said Holly. "But... Well, the thing is that I was cleaning out my attic recently, getting rid of some of Eric's old stuff."

"Like his Legos," Odelia said encouragingly.

"Like his Legos," Holly agreed. "And so I found this box I'd totally forgotten that I still had. You see, after Eric had his accident, the police came by the house and dropped off this box with the stuff he had on him when he was... well, when he died." Her mom had placed a hand on her arm as she wrestled to tell the story. "At the time, I simply didn't have the courage to go through it. But now I figured I'd better make short shrift of it and throw away what I didn't need anymore. And I found his cell phone, so I decided to see if it still worked, since it was brand-new when he bought it four years ago. So I plugged it in and it recharged just fine. But when I looked, I saw that there were a bunch of messages on his phone that... well, they weren't from me but from some other woman. And these messages, they were pretty..." She swallowed again. "They were very..."

"Eric was having an affair," her mom said. "With some other woman."

"Norma Parkman," said Holly.

"She's the butcher's wife," her mom supplied.

"So I confronted Norma. Told her that I knew about her and Eric. I even showed her the phone and the messages. She got very upset and said that it had been nothing but a brief fling and it hadn't meant anything. I wanted to believe her, but when I checked the messages, they went back months, so their fling wasn't as brief as Norma wanted me to believe. But when I confronted her, she said I was mistaken and that as far as she was concerned, the matter was closed. I was the only person in the shop, but then her husband walked in and I could tell that she became really uncomfortable."

"Of course she did," Mr. Williams said with a shake of his head.

"So she more or less ushered me out, and as I walked out of the shop, she followed me and practically begged me not to tell her husband. She said that she'd suffered a moment of weakness but that her marriage was back on track and that she didn't want her husband to know. I told her I had no intention of telling anyone, but it was obvious she didn't believe me. So now I'm thinking..."

"You're thinking that maybe Norma Parkman paid Antoine O'Neil to break in and find your husband's phone," Odelia supplied.

Holly nodded. "The thought has just occurred to me when you mentioned this woman and the 'untold riches.' For her, that phone probably does represent a great prize. If she can make it go away, it would prevent the truth from ever coming out since I wouldn't be able to prove a thing and it would be her word against mine."

"But you told her you wouldn't tell Mikel!" said her mom.

"Obviously, Norma didn't believe her," Mr. Williams said. "And to be honest, I probably wouldn't believe her either." He shrugged. "In her mind, she probably thought 'better safe than sorry' and paid off this guy to steal that phone."

"We'll have a chat with Mrs. Parkman," Chase promised. "Do you still have the phone, or was it stolen?"

"I put it in my safe at the bank," said Holly. "No idea why. After I talked to Norma, I just had this idea that I probably shouldn't keep it at the house."

"Good thinking," said her mom. "Always follow your instincts, honey."

"So the guy didn't find that phone the first time," said her dad. "So he came back a second night. Only this time he and his drug addict buddy got into a fight, and one of them ended up dead. Is that what happened, do you think?"

"It's very likely," Chase admitted.

From across the kitchen, a familiar dog now came tripping up to us. It was, of course, Babette, newly reunited with her humans. "So what's all this about a drug addict breaking into our home?" she asked. And so we told her the whole story. Deep down, I hoped it would dissuade her from pursuing the ghost story angle, but if anything, it strengthened her resolve. "You have to get rid of this ghost, Max," she said seriously. "These drug addicts have a very negative vibe. It's going to make our home absolutely unlivable from now on. So you have to go and talk to him and persuade him to leave. And since he will only leave once you have solved his murder, that's what you'll have to do first."

"I know," I said. I was starting to regret having agreed to this whole ghost business.

"So what happens if we meet a bonobo, Babette?" asked Dooley. "Do we also ask him to leave? Because bonobos can get very aggressive, you know. They're like geese. They don't like people trespassing on their territory."

Babette stared at my friend. "Bonobos? Geese? What are you talking about, Dooley?"

"It's all right," I said. "It's just code for ghosts."

"No, it's not," said Dooley. "If Max is going to get rid of these bonobos for you, you have to understand it's going to prove very dangerous." He frowned. "So how did they get into your home, exactly? Did they escape from the zoo?"

Babette turned to me, and I gave her a short shake of the head. When Dooley was entertaining his own theories and hypotheses, it was better not to engage. And since Babette essentially is a very clever dog, in spite of her miniature size, she gave me a smile of understanding and told Dooley, "When you see a bonobo, back away slowly, Dooley. They are big, they are probably angry, and they'll squash you like a bug."

Dooley gulped. "Yikes," he said. "But I don't want to be squashed like a bug!"

"That's why you have to back away slowly. Especially when you encounter the ghost of a bonobo. They're even worse than their living counterparts."

"A bonobo ghost!" Dooley cried.

Babette patted him on the head. "It's all right. Max will protect you. Isn't that right, Max?"

"Mh? Oh, absolutely. I'll protect you from any ghost, whether of the bonobo or the human variety. In fact, I might even open my own ghost-hunting agency soon, getting rid of all manner of ghosts."

Babette smiled. "I knew you'd start to see things my way, Max. Consider this a test run of your new ghost-hunting agency. Get rid of the ghost of Antoine O'Neil, and everything will be smooth sailing from here on out. Just wait and see."

Somehow I had my doubts about that, but I decided to refrain from voicing them. After all, a customer is a customer, whether pro bono or not.

CHAPTER 14

I have to say, I didn't mind paying a visit to a butcher shop. After all, butcher shops are very popular with the feline crowd as a rule. You might even say that butchers feature in our personal top ten favorite shops. Humans might prefer flower shops or bakeries or boutiques, but not cats. Give us fishmongers and butchers over bakers and florists any day. But since this wasn't a social call, and I had a feeling that the butcher's wife wouldn't appreciate our presence if Chase and Odelia were going to start hurling accusations her way, I didn't hold high hopes of receiving any special meaty treats.

Though when we walked into the shop, those delicious smells almost made me pass out.

"Wow, this is a great place," said Dooley the moment the door had closed behind us. "I mean, look at this stuff, Max!"

And look at the stuff I most certainly did: sausages, legs of lamb, beefsteaks, pork chops, chicken fillets... This place was paradise!

We both had a hard time focusing on the matter at hand, and so when the butcher's wife walked into the store, wearing a warm smile on her face and clearly eager to serve her customers, I almost missed the opening strands of the conversation. With a supreme effort, I dragged my mind back from roseate dreams of making a home in that meat display counter and living there forever, and concentrated on the interaction between our humans and the purveyor of all those goodies.

They say cats don't easily fall in love, but for some reason, I experienced a powerful sensation of love at first sight when I laid eyes on Norma Parkman. In some ways, she reminded me of Scarlett Canyon, in the sense that she, too, had an abundance of assets on display. But whereas in Scarlett's case, what you see is what you get, and everything is as nature intended it to be, in Mrs. Parkman's case, she must have employed a small team of plastic surgeons to achieve her remarkable appearance. From her chest to her face, a lot of work had gone into those looks. But none of that mattered. The woman was in the meat business, and that was enough for us to see her through rose-tinted glasses.

Chase had flashed his badge, and so had Odelia, and the kindly smile the woman had displayed was instantly replaced with one of a certain dread.

"Let's talk outside," she said curtly, with a touch of sudden coldness, and proceeded to turn around the 'Closed' sign on the door and walk out of the shop, followed by her surprised and unwelcome visitors. Her high heels made click-clacking sounds on the pavement, and when she felt she had put enough distance between herself and the shop—or more likely her husband—she halted and turned to face us. "So what is this all about?" she asked, crossing her arms across her chest. Though from her demeanor, I think it was clear she knew exactly what this was about.

"We have it on good authority," said Chase, opening the proceedings, "that you hired a man named Antoine O'Neil to steal a phone from Holly Mitchell by breaking into her house. When he failed to retrieve the item the first time around, he returned the next night for a second attempt, at which point he was shot at point-blank range and died on Mrs. Mitchell's kitchen floor."

The woman blinked her pair of extended lashes and pursed her unnaturally puffy lips.

"She looks like a duck, Max," said Dooley.

"That's why we call this a duckface, Dooley," I said. "It's because of all the lip fillers she injected into her lips." Though it was probably safer to say she had paid someone to do the honors, just as she had paid Mr. O'Neil for his services.

"I have no idea what you're talking about," she said.

"You and Eric Mitchell had an affair," Odelia explained. "As evidenced by the text messages on Eric's phone. A phone his wife discovered a couple of days ago and confronted you with. At which point you decided to retrieve the phone by any means possible and hired Antoine O'Neil. We have both the phone with the messages and a witness who confirms that Mr. O'Neil was hired by you."

Technically speaking, they had neither the phone nor a positive ID of the mystery woman who had approached Toby Grave. But Norma didn't know that. And since she was convinced that Odelia was telling the truth, she unpuckered her lips and suddenly seemed to slump a little.

"I didn't kill him, if that's what you're implying," she said. "All I did was pay the guy to get that phone for me. That's not a crime, is it?"

"Oh, I think you'll find that it is," Chase said. "Paying someone to break into a person's home to steal their personal property? You're in big trouble, Mrs. Parkman."

In spite of her high heels, she succumbed to the combined effects of gravity and a guilty conscience a little more and now presented a pitiful sight. She couldn't frown or display any kind of emotion because of all the Botox, but her eyes could still shed tears as her tear ducts hadn't been frozen like the rest of her face, and she now shed them freely. "Are you going to arrest me?" she asked in a tremulous voice.

"Just tell us what happened," said Odelia, adopting a gentler tone. She even went so far as to retrieve a tissue from her pocket and hand it to the butcher's wife.

"Okay, so I had the affair with Eric Mitchell. It all started when he came into the shop to order a steak. He said my steaks were the juiciest he had ever seen. And then he ordered some chicken legs and told me that my legs—"

"Were the best he had ever seen," said Chase. "Yes, I think we get the picture, Mrs. Parkman."

"He openly flirted with me, but in such a charming way that I found him irresistible. I knew he was married, of course, and he knew I was too. But that didn't stop us from starting an affair. It was just supposed to be a bit of fun, you know. Nothing serious. But as the weeks turned into months, and we were still seeing each other, we both realized we had passed the frivolous fun stage a long time ago, and things were starting to get really serious between us. But then Eric died in that accident, and suddenly it was all over. For weeks I lived in fear that his wife would find out and tell my husband, but when nothing happened, I started to relax, figuring the whole thing was behind me. Until a couple of days ago when she suddenly turned up and showed me Eric's phone. Apparently, she hadn't looked at it when the police had handed it back to her, but now she had, and discovered our affair. I begged her not to tell Mikel, and even though she said she wouldn't, I knew that phone would hang over my head like the sword of Damocles for the rest of my life, and I decided I couldn't live like that."

"So you went to the park and asked some random homeless person to steal that phone for you?"

"Pretty much," said Norma. "I'd seen them hanging around the downtown area and also the park, and a friend of mine had said something about the number of break-ins having risen precipitously since they arrived in town. So that got me thinking. Who would be surprised by another break-in? No one. Not even the police would think twice when another home was burgled by one of these people looking for money to fund their habit. So I screwed up my courage, went down to the park, and approached the first person I saw. They referred me to Antoine, who they said had a criminal record. Antoine immediately agreed. So I paid him what he wanted, gave him the address, and agreed to meet again so he could hand me the phone. Only when I returned to the park yesterday morning, he said he hadn't found the phone."

"So he returned last night," said Odelia. "Only this time things turned ugly."

"Look, I know I shouldn't have paid the guy to steal that phone. But I was desperate. Holly had given me a real fright."

"Can you blame her? She just discovered that her husband was having an affair with you. I think she handled herself remarkably well. By the same token, she could have attacked you or told your husband."

"I know, and I'm sorry," said Norma. "But I didn't kill Antoine, if that's what you're thinking. Why would I? He was my only hope to get that phone back and destroy the evidence of my affair before my husband found out."

"Can you tell us where you were last night around eight?" asked Chase.

"Home, watching television with Mikel," she said. "But please don't ask him. He'll want to know why, and then you're probably obliged to tell him, right?"

"Not necessarily," said Odelia, who clearly felt sorry for the woman. "But we will have to verify your alibi, Mrs. Parkman."

"If Mikel finds out…" She bit her lip. "He's a good man and the perfect husband, apart from one thing: he's insanely jealous. Even if a customer looks at me a certain way, he'll get upset."

"He'll probably have a lot of opportunity to get upset, Max," said Dooley. "Since Mrs. Parkman probably has a lot of success with the male element."

I grinned. "Yes, I would say she has."

"I really had nothing to do with the death of that man," Norma assured us.

"Can you think of anyone who would?" asked Odelia.

She thought for a moment. "Well, it is no secret that Holly Mitchell isn't well-liked in this neighborhood. So maybe whoever killed Antoine really intended to kill Holly? Just an idea."

"Holly isn't well-liked? But why?"

"Well, all of us are part of the same group, you see."

"The neighborhood watch, you mean?"

"Not the watch, no. The WhatsApp group. The whole street has joined the same WhatsApp group, and we like to organize activities, but mostly we coordinate our dog walks. The only person who refuses to join is Holly. I don't know why, but rumor has it she's too stuck up to want to associate with the rest of us. It's created a lot of bad blood between her and her neighbors, most of who actively hate her."

"Like who?" asked Chase.

"There's Mark Cooper," said Norma, clearly happy to deflect attention away from herself. "He lives across the street from Holly. I'm not sure what it's all about, but he's always complaining about parking space."

"Parking space?"

"That's right. Won't shut up about it. And then there's Mae West, who lives next door to Holly. They have been locked in a long-time dispute over Mae's cherry tree."

"A cherry tree," said Chase, arching a skeptical eyebrow.

"Ask Mae. She'll tell you all about it."

"I can imagine she will," said the cop, though he seemed reluctant to broach the subject with the woman, for fear of getting an earful in return.

"Do you own a gun, Mrs. Parkman?" asked Odelia.

"No, I don't."

"Your husband?"

She hesitated a moment too long. "He owns a rifle," she finally admitted. "But not a handgun. Why? You don't think Mikel..." Her eyes suddenly widened, and she brought a distraught hand to her face. "You don't think..."

"What are the chances that your husband found out about your affair?"

"Could he have overheard you and Holly discussing this phone business?" Chase supplied.

"It's always possible," Norma admitted. "We were talking in the shop, and even though Mikel mostly confines himself to the area behind the shop, it's always possible that... Oh, my God. You don't think he..."

"I'm afraid we'll have to ask him, Mrs. Parkman," said Chase.

"So it might be better if you told him about the affair before we do," Odelia said.

"But why? Why would he go after Antoine? He'd have no reason to."

"Maybe he thought that you were also having an affair with Antoine?" Chase suggested.

Norma barked an incredulous laugh. "Did you see the guy? He wasn't exactly Christian Grey." She shook her head. "The only reason I approached him was because he promised he could get me that phone, nothing more."

"But your husband didn't know that. Maybe he followed

you to the park and saw you and Antoine talking and started following the man around."

She sighed. "I'm going to have to tell him, aren't I?"

"I'm afraid so," Odelia said.

"He's going to blow a gasket," she said. But she seemed to realize she had no other choice and nodded. "Fine. I'll tell him tonight. But I can tell you right now that Mikel is not your guy. The man might look like a tank, but deep down he's a pussycat. Though after what I have to say, he might turn into a tiger."

CHAPTER 15

Since clearly Odelia and Chase felt there's no time like the present, they decided to tackle these accusations about neighborly disputes first. And so our next port of call was Mark Cooper, who did indeed live right across the street from Holly. We recognized him from the park, where he had been handing out flyers the night before, and we also recognized the poodle who appeared behind him.

"Oh, it's so great to see you again," said Melvin.

"It is?" I said, much surprised. The last time we met Melvin hadn't been all that happy to see us.

"Since we talked last night I asked around, and turns out you guys are the greatest detectives that ever lived. And for another, your human is not too shabby either. And also, you're friends with Rufus and Fifi from dog choir, so that tells me all I need to know to welcome you into my humble home!"

"That's great," I said, relaxing. "So you are a member of dog choir, are you?"

"Guilty as charged!" said the gray-haired poodle. "And having a blast, too. So have you found out what's going on?

Who killed that man across the street and how? Was it some exotic poison that was slipped into the victim's soup? Or a knife stuck between his ribs that mysteriously vanished without a trace? I, too, am an avid consumer of mystery tales, you see. And so is Mark. In fact, all we watch are mystery shows, and all Mark reads are mystery books." And to show us he wasn't kidding, he took us to a large book rack with hundreds of books neatly positioned according to topic and author, and as far as I could tell, all of them were devoted to the mystery and crime genre.

"Well, the thing is that a little birdie told us that your human has some kind of beef going on with Holly Mitchell," I said as I studied the titles on display.

"The butcher's wife told us," Dooley revealed. "She thinks that Mark might have had something to do with the death of that man in Holly's house last night."

"Mark! Oh, he would never do something like that," Melvin said. "Never, never, never. Mark may adore crime fiction, but that doesn't mean he's a killer!"

"But he does know an awful lot about crime, I gather," I said, finding myself intrigued by a thick tome that claimed to be 'The World's Biggest Book on Very Effective Murder Methods.'

"Oh, he does. If he wanted to, he could easily become a consultant to the police. But like I said, he would never raise his hand in anger against another human being. Or a dog, for that matter. Or any species, really."

"So what's all this about a beef with Holly Mitchell?" I asked.

"It's just a minor thing," said Melvin. "When Mark moved into this house many moons ago, it was with the understanding that the spot in front of the house was his designated parking spot, and so he's been parking his car there for years. Only when Holly and her husband moved in a couple of years ago, they decided to take Mark's spot, since they can't park in front of their house, on account of the planters the city council has put there to bring more green to the streets. You'll see them at regular intervals now, all along the street. Only they took away parking spots, of course."

"Of course."

"And then there are the spots that are reserved for the handicapped, and also the spots where only electric vehicles can park, next to one of those charging stations. All in all, about thirty percent of parking spaces has disappeared over time. And since Holly and Eric felt that they should be able to park close to their house, as many people do, they started parking in front of our house."

"And Mark doesn't agree."

"Mark does not agree at all. But Holly claims there are no designated parking spots, so she can park wherever she likes. Whereas Mark feels that there's an implicit understanding that this spot is his. And so they argue."

"And have argued for years, apparently."

"They have, and very vociferously, too."

"So who's winning the war?" asked Dooley.

"So far it's a toss-up, I'd say," said Melvin. "Lately, Mark has adopted a new method, whereby he will permanently park his car in the same spot and not move it."

"But that means he can't use his car."

"He doesn't mind. To him, it's more important to assert his right than any practical problems this might pose to him."

"But... how does he get around if he can't drive his car?"

"He walks. And he's also bought himself an electric bicycle."

It seemed a little odd to me that Mark would be so adamant to exert this so-called 'right' of his that he would inconvenience himself to such an extent. But it must be true, for the conversation between our humans and Mark, snatches of which reached our ears while we stood talking to Melvin, confirmed that here was a man who felt very strongly about his inalienable right to park where he had parked for years.

"He wouldn't... murder over it, would he?" I asked finally.

Melvin laughed a pleasant laugh. "Oh, Max. Murder? Of course not! Why would he have to murder anyone? His car is parked exactly where he wants it, and so he's a happy man. In fact, since he's developed this novel and quite revolutionary method of exercising his right to occupy a section of the public domain, he's never been happier."

"Even though he can't use his car anymore."

"He's using his bicycle, which is even better! Better for his overall health, better for the environment, and better for his wallet, since he doesn't have to buy gas."

"But... he still has to pay motor vehicle tax and safety inspections. So why doesn't he simply sell it?"

"And give up his parking space? Never!"

"Okay," I said, seeing that Melvin was just as fanatic about his parking spot as his human was. "You wouldn't be able to tell us where Mark was last night around eight, would you?"

"I know exactly where he was. Right here with me on the couch watching a rerun of *Murder She Wrote*, immediately followed by new episodes of *CSI: Vegas* and *NCIS*, and to top it off, we watched an old episode of *Columbo* and a documentary about Dahmer. All in all, a very instructive evening, Max."

"I'll bet," I said. But if the dog said it was so, I guess it was true.

Meanwhile, the interview with Mark seemed to be drawing to its conclusion, and as we caught the tail end of it, I marveled once again at the stubbornness of a man willing to sacrifice his mobility and comfort just to score a point against a neighbor.

"So you have never seen this man before?" Chase was asking as he showed Mark a picture of the dead man.

Mark studied it intensely. "He was shot, I read. What caliber gun was used? Are you at liberty to tell me, Detective Kingsley?"

"No, I'm sorry, but I'm not," said Chase. "As this investigation is ongoing, we can't divulge that information, I'm afraid."

"Mh," said the guy. "They must have used a silencer, or otherwise someone would have heard. And by someone, I'm referring to Mae and Julio West, of course, who live right next door and whose kitchen shares a wall with the Mitchell kitchen. Though Mae mostly spends her evenings gardening while Julio watches whatever game is on, so it's entirely possible they didn't hear. Which presents us with an interesting conundrum, doesn't it?"

"It does?" asked Chase, staring at the man.

"Well, yes, of course. How did Antoine O'Neil enter the house without being seen by Mae? Because, as you may or may not know, Mae has eyes in the back of her head. And nothing goes on in Holly's backyard that Mae hasn't seen."

"And why is that?" asked Odelia. "Because of the cherry tree?"

Mark nodded approvingly. "I see you have done your homework, Mrs. Kingsley. Yes, exactly because of that cherry tree. For as long as I can remember, a dispute has raged over that tree. You see, the branches mostly extend over the hedge into the Mitchell backyard, and so the cherries drop there, or at least over seventy percent of them, at last count. So naturally, the Wests don't feel it's right for those cherries to land in Holly's backyard and be eaten by Holly's kids and Holly herself. They even thought about taking her to court, but I advised them against it, as lawyers are expensive."

"I'm pretty sure that if those cherries fall into Holly's

backyard, they're hers to pick up," said Chase. "At least in New York, that is the case. Other states might have other ideas, but as far as I know, that's the law."

"I very much doubt that, Detective," said Mark. "That just can't be true. It doesn't seem fair."

"It would be better if the Wests and Holly talked to each other," Odelia suggested. "And worked out some kind of solution. And the same goes for you, Mr. Cooper. I mean, you can't even use your car right now."

The man's features darkened into an expression of disgust. "There's simply no way to talk to that woman. Oh, I've tried, believe me, I've tried. But she's so flippant in her responses it borders on sheer arrogance. So I've simply given up. And besides..." He forced a smile. "I've rediscovered cycling, and it's proving to be a real boon to my overall health. So there's your silver lining right there!"

CHAPTER 16

*W*e found Mae West in her modest little front garden, rooting out pesky weeds. Of her husband Julio there was no trace, as he had headed into town to do a little shopping. Mrs. West was a cheerful woman of about sixty, with a round face and a pleasant demeanor. She certainly didn't strike me as the type of person who would go to court over a couple of cherries, but then stranger things have happened, of course. Next to her, an Alsatian lay reposing peacefully, though the moment we approached, he pricked up his ears and became attentive.

"Maybe I should leave my cats in the car," said Odelia as she gave the large dog a look.

"Oh, nonsense," said Mrs. West. "Roger Moore wouldn't hurt a fly. Now what is it you wanted to talk about? The dead man next door, presumably?"

"That, and your cherry," said Chase.

The woman's cheeks reddened. "I beg your pardon?"

Chase realized his social faux pas and hastened to clarify, "Your cherry *tree*. According to several testimonies from your neighbors, you and Mrs. Mitchell don't get along due to a conflict about a cherry tree?"

"Oh, that," said Mrs. West with a casual wave of the hand. "That's all taken care of. Julio and I have decided to cut that tree at the root. Problem solved."

"You're going to cut your cherry tree?"

"That's right. Ever since we planted that tree and it first began to produce fruit, it's been the same story every year. Unfortunately for us, we planted it much too close to the fence, and so now over seventy percent of the tree actually hangs over that woman's side. And since she figures that every cherry that falls into her backyard is hers, she brazenly picks them up and eats them! She even bakes cherry pie and then has the gall to offer us a piece." She shook her head. "She's the worst neighbor you can imagine. Too bad Mrs. Pecker decided to move, for she was the perfect neighbor. Never had any trouble with her. She also picked up the cherries, but then handed them back to us—to the last one!"

"And now you're going to cut it down?" asked Odelia. "That seems like such a pity. Can't you talk things through with Holly?"

"Absolutely not. We have tried talking to her until we were blue in the face, but she will not budge. She's adamant that those cherries are rightfully hers, and so she will pick them—and eat them!"

As the conversation flowed back and forth between Mae and our humans, we turned our attention to Roger Moore, who was still eyeing us with keen attention.

"Say, have I met you guys before?" he asked now.

"It's possible," I said.

"Are you a member of dog choir, Roger Moore?" asked Dooley. "Because we spend a lot of time at the park, which is where we may have met."

"I'm not a member, unfortunately," said Roger Moore.

"Though I would like to join. But Melvin keeps telling me I don't have a great singing voice, and apparently that's one of the major requirements to join up." He gave us a sad look. "I have been taking lessons, you know. Practicing my scales, but it's no good. I can practice all I want, but I'll never be a great singer. Not like Melvin."

"I think you will find that the most important aspect of dog choir, and by extension also cat choir, is not that you're an ace singer," I told the dog. "But that you enjoy spending time with other dogs."

"Yeah, we have a friend who can't sing either," said Dooley. "And yet she's the first soprano of cat choir."

"As strange as this may sound, it's not about the singing," I told Roger Moore.

"It isn't?" asked the dog, very much surprised.

"Of course not. So tonight you simply go to the park and ask to join, and I'm sure Fifi and Rufus will let you."

"You know Fifi and Rufus?"

"They're our neighbors," I said.

"Oh, goodie," said the dog. "Oh, goodie, goodie, goodie! Oh, joy!"

"So can we ask you a couple of questions?" I asked.

"Shoot!" said the dog, looking very happy that he would be able to join his friends at dog choir. "Ask me anything you like, Max. You have made me so happy!"

"Okay, so I don't know if you know this, but last night a man was killed next door."

"Yeah, I heard all about that," said the Alsatian. "Sad business. Very sad."

"Do you think that your humans may have had any involvement in that?"

He frowned at me. "I don't understand the question."

"Well, your humans have been locked in this conflict over the cherry tree, right?"

"Right."

"So do you think it's possible that Julio or Mae finally decided that enough was enough, and so they went over to Holly's house with a gun, wanting to have it out with her once and for all? Only when they arrived there, they didn't find Holly but Antoine O'Neil. There was an altercation and either Mae or Julio ended up shooting the man. Is that a likely scenario, would you say?"

Roger Moore smiled. "Oh, Max. You are funny, aren't you? Mae or Julio shooting a person in cold blood? Of course not! Impossible! They may not get along with Holly over that cherry tree, but that doesn't mean they're going to become violent."

"Did you happen to see anything last night?" asked Dooley now. "Or hear something?"

"Like what?" asked Roger Moore.

"Well, like some kind of fight," I said. "Loud words being spoken. The sound of a shot fired."

He thought about this for a moment but finally had to admit defeat. "No, I'm afraid I didn't hear anything of the kind. No fight, no loud words being spoken, and definitely not the sound of a shot being fired." He seemed genuinely sorry. "I would very much like to help you, but that's how it is."

"It's all right," I said. "It seemed like a long shot, but I figured we had to ask."

"Oh, of course. Like I said, you can ask me anything."

"Well, as a matter of fact…" I had developed an appetite, and seeing as dog kibble isn't all that different from cat kibble, a minor snack might tide me over nicely. "Could we have a bit to eat, maybe?" I asked therefore. Odelia probably wouldn't approve, but then she was too busy talking to Mae to notice.

And since Roger Moore was clearly a very nice dog, he

led us inside, where he presented us with a choice of no less than three different bowls filled with three different kinds of kibble. And since I had a hard time choosing, I decided to sample all three choices. And I had to say all of them were excellent.

I glanced out through the window at the backyard, where I saw that famous cherry tree, large and majestic, and wondered if there really was no other solution than to cut it down. It seemed like such a sad fate for that poor tree. And all because a couple of neighbors couldn't get along.

"Are you friends with Babette?" I asked.

"Oh, absolutely. We get along great. In fact, all the dogs in this neighborhood get along well. Melvin and Babette and Mike... We see each other all the time at the dog park. There's a WhatsApp group, you see, and our humans are all big fans."

"Except for Holly," I pointed out.

"Yes, I guess she's the odd one out."

"Any idea why?"

"Well, I asked Babette, of course, and she says it's because Holly got upset when her husband died four years ago. You see, the neighborhood wanted to do something for her when they found out what happened. So they all got together and decided to organize a sort of wake. We would all gather in the park and people would burn candles and read poems in honor of Eric's death. But when they suggested it to Holly, she bridled. Said she didn't think it was a good idea and basically told them to can it. And since then there's been this tension between her and the neighborhood."

"But why? Why didn't she think this wake was a good idea?"

"According to Babette, it has to do with the fact that Eric was having an affair with a neighbor. Only Holly didn't know which neighbor, and so she more or less lumped them all together."

"Holly knew that Eric was having an affair with one of her neighbors?"

"She did. Apparently, she had discovered text messages on her husband's phone that proved that he was having an affair. Only she had no idea who those messages were from. Both Eric and this other woman used aliases. He was Superman and she was Lois Lane. But the messages were pretty hot. Hot enough to make her skin crawl. So she showed them to Mae, back when they were still on speaking terms, but Mae said she had no idea. And when Holly asked some of the other neighbors, they all claimed not to know who this Lois Lane could possibly be. In the end, she gave up and figured they all knew perfectly well who her husband's mistress was, but they were protecting her."

"How did she know she was one of their neighbors?"

"Because they kept referring to their daily dog walk. Superman would meet Lois Lane at the dog park. So logically, it had to be someone from around here. And since pretty much all the neighbors here have dogs, and they all go to the dog park, it stood to reason that they must have seen the two lovers together and must have known but were keeping quiet to protect the identity of this woman."

"And that's how the relationship between Holly and her neighbors soured."

Roger Moore nodded. "Such a pity, too, for Holly is certainly a nice lady."

"Do you think the neighborhood knew who Lois Lane was?" I asked.

"Of course, they did. It's Norma Parkman. I saw Eric and Norma together all the time, schmoozing and kissing when they thought nobody was looking. Very lovey-dovey."

"So why didn't they tell Holly when she asked?"

"Because they didn't want to cause trouble. Holly would have accused Norma, and then Norma's husband would have found out, and it would have led to this huge blow-up that nobody wanted. So they felt more comfortable pretending it never happened, figuring it would go away after Eric died."

"But it didn't."

"Oh, the rumors of the affair died down, of course. But the enmity between Holly and her neighbors never went away. On the contrary, I get the impression they like each other less now than they did before. With the cherry tree and Mark Cooper from across the street over his parking spot. And Chris Goldsworthy over his offer to buy Holly's property and her refusing even to consider it."

Now that was one I hadn't heard before. "Chris Goldsworthy wants to buy Holly's house?"

"Absolutely. He's her other next-door neighbor, you see, and has been wanting to expand for years. If he could buy Holly's house, he could knock out a couple of walls and create one big place for himself and his family. But Holly won't sell."

"Interesting," I said. "Why, thanks, Roger Moore. You certainly are a fount of information."

"Only too happy to help, Max. After all, you finally got me into dog choir!"

CHAPTER 17

While Dooley and I were talking to Roger Moore, Chase and Odelia had finished interviewing Mae West. Apparently, her alibi was that she and her husband had spent the evening inside watching television. When asked what they had watched, Mae said they had watched a Roger Moore movie, which was appropriate since they had named their dog after the well-known actor. What was more important, though, was that Roger Moore himself confirmed to us that his humans had been on the couch with him perched right between them.

"I love Roger Moore movies," he confessed. "I can watch them all the time."

"Is that why they called you what they called you?" I asked.

"That's right," said the Alsatian. "How did you know?"

"Just a hunch."

"When I was a pup and they didn't know what to name me, every time a Roger Moore movie came on, I would start to bark, so they figured I liked the man's movies. And so that's what they called me."

I had the impression that we had arrived in a household where they all loved Mr. Moore—both the man and the dog. Who they didn't like was Holly Mitchell, but at least now we were starting to get an idea why that was. But when I told Odelia, she said Holly had lied to us, which I guess she had, and decided to have another chat with her.

At least now we also knew why the Wests or their dog hadn't heard a gunshot: Bond movies are usually filled with plenty of gunshots of their own, as well as the odd explosion, so an extra one sounding from next door would have been drowned out by the noise.

Before we talked to Holly again, first we needed to talk to Christopher Goldsworthy and discuss his future plans for Holly's house. The man opened the door dressed in flowery Bermuda shorts and an equally flowery shirt. He was a middle-aged man who looked very trim and healthy for his age, and when I saw the pair of tongs in his hand, I knew we were in for a treat.

"I was just firing up the grill," he told us. "Come on in and have a bite to eat, detectives!"

And even though technically I'm not a detective, and the invitation presumably wasn't intended for us, I still was the first one in and making a beeline for the backyard, where presumably this great feast was in progress. Much to my disappointment, no delicious smells wafted my way, and when I finally arrived at my destination, I saw that the man hadn't lied: he had only recently started up that grill, and no meat was ready for my appreciation.

Dooley looked equally disappointed. "Where is the food, Max?" he asked.

"No idea, but it's not here," I told him.

Odelia and Chase, who looked mildly embarrassed by my and Dooley's alacrity in locating the good stuff, profusely apologized to Mr. Goldsworthy.

"Oh, it's fine," the man said laughingly. "Bruno is exactly the same way. The moment he sniffs out something to eat, there's no holding him back."

"Bruno is your dog?" asked Chase.

"Yeah, he's a Dalmatian. My wife just took him for a stroll."

"Just our luck," I grumbled. "The dog isn't here to talk to us, and there's no food anywhere in sight." But since there was nothing else to do but to settle in and wait until the interview was over, we chose a spot conveniently close to the grill and hoped that Mr. Goldsworthy would get a move on and supply us with some tasty morsels before we had to leave.

"So we talked to some of your neighbors," Odelia said, opening the proceedings, "and they all told us the same story: there seems to be some kind of beef going on between Holly Mitchell and her neighbors. And it all goes back to an affair her husband Eric was having with a woman who called herself Lois Lane."

Mr. Goldsworthy eyed her with unveiled admiration. "You found out all of that by talking to my neighbors? Congratulations. I didn't think they would divulge the affair to you."

"You were planning to keep it a secret, is that it?" asked Chase.

"Well, it isn't our secret to share," Mr. Goldsworthy pointed out. He was still waving those tongs, and I closely followed his every move, keeping my eyes peeled. "Look, when the Mitchells moved in next door, I think we were all keen to welcome them to the neighborhood. And they seemed like a nice enough couple. I organized a barbecue in their honor, the whole neighborhood came out, and for a while there, it looked like we would all get along splendidly. But then Eric started his affair, his wife found out, and things have soured a lot since then. Holly seems to blame us for not telling her about the affair, and then some minor disagreements started cropping up, and generally the atmosphere now resembles that of a cold war. Even though it was never our intention it would come to this."

"Is it true that you want to buy Holly's house, and she's refusing to sell?" asked Chase.

The man seemed taken aback by the question, but he quickly recovered. "Well, yes. Who told you?"

"Oh, just a little birdie," said Chase. "So you put in an offer, and she turned you down?"

He shrugged. "Look, I got married late in life, my wife being twenty years my junior, and even though I never expected it, I'm now blessed with a family of five, and so obviously this house is getting too small for us. Naturally, I started looking for options to expand. We could sell this place and move to a bigger house, but we all like it here. This neighborhood is our home. We know everybody, and our neighbors aren't just neighbors, they're friends. And that's not even a cliché. It's the reality."

"Except Holly."

"Yes, except Holly. So I decided to offer to buy her house, figuring she'd be happy to get out since she doesn't like us and she doesn't like the neighborhood. Imagine my surprise when she turned me down flat. And not just once, but multiple times, since I kept coming back with higher and higher offers, figuring she felt I wasn't giving her the market value for the place, which I did, by the way."

"So last night, did you hear anything out of the ordinary? Or see anything?"

"Didn't see a thing, didn't hear a thing."

"No gunshot? Nobody clambering over the fence?"

"Nope. Nothing."

"Where were you, Mr. Goldsworthy?"

"Right here at home, with my wife and kids. Ask them—they'll confirm it."

The man seemed sincere enough, I thought. And if we bumped into the dog and he told us this was so, I guess that was case closed and another potential suspect eliminated from our inquiries. But when Chase and Odelia made to leave, I won't conceal the fact that I experienced a certain disappointment. After all, when one's hopes have been built up, and you fully expect a nice morsel of meat in your immediate future, and then you don't get it—it's very frustrating!

Then again, such is life as a detective, I guess. Plenty of shoe leather but no food. And if you tell me that we ate at Roger Moore's place, then I'll come right back and tell you it's better to have small bites all of the time than one big meal some of the time. That's my life philosophy and I'll stand by it.

CHAPTER 18

One of the main problems with being a detective is that it's so time-consuming. You interview a number of people, be they suspects or witnesses or whatnot, and if you're lucky, they will answer your questions truthfully and you're done. Unfortunately, this is mostly not the case. People will either tell you a blatant lie or they will try to get away with spreading half-truths. Sooner or later, you will discover that you have been lied to, and you will have to go back and interview those people again. And again, and again!

And so it was with Holly Mitchell. No sooner had we talked to the woman than we sat down with her in the pleasant kitchen of her parents' home once more. And since at this point I was pretty much starving, it only took one word from Babette for Dooley and me to empty her bowl and look around for more. Odelia didn't like it, I could tell, but then she should have brought along a packed lunch for us. You can't expect a feline to function on fumes, can you?

"Thanks, Babette," I said gratefully. "That hit the spot."

"I knew you were starving, Max," the teacup Chihuahua

said. "I could see that your circumference had dropped a few inches around the waist."

I patted my waist with satisfaction. "I think the problem has been remedied now. I feel like I can go for another couple of hours of these interviews—no problem!" I then turned to Babette. "You haven't been entirely honest with us, Babette."

"I haven't?"

"Roger Moore told us that Holly knew all along that her husband was having an affair with one of their neighbors. She just didn't know which neighbor. You should have told us."

She sighed deeply. "It's a fine line to tread, fellas, between assisting a pair of fellow pets in their inquiries and protecting one's human's privacy. To be honest, I didn't think it was all that important."

"Not important! It may very well be the most important aspect of this case!"

"I don't see how. Okay, so Eric had an affair and Holly found out about it. What does that have to do with a man being found murdered in our kitchen? This affair was four years ago, Max. We have all moved on since then. No, I really think this is a wild-goose chase on your part, and you'd do much better focusing on figuring out what that man was doing in our kitchen and who shot him and why."

I would have argued with her that the affair was important, but an interesting conversation was taking place overhead, and I decided to tune in.

"Okay, so I knew about the affair," Holly confessed. This time her mom and dad were absent from the scene, as presumably they had their own lives to live and weren't their daughter's keepers. "I didn't know who the woman was, though."

"Did you confront your husband with the evidence?"

"I would have, but I only found out a couple of days before he was killed. At first, I found it very hard to believe that he could do such a thing, and then when I finally decided to confront him about it, he was gone." She was silent for a moment, reliving those awful days. Then she looked up. "I quickly figured out that whoever this woman was, she had to be one of our neighbors since they frequently mentioned the dog park in their messages. Apparently, it was one of the places they used to meet. And since the dog park isn't exactly a private area, someone must have seen them together. So I asked Mae West about it, but she said she had no idea. I could tell she was lying, though. And when I asked some of the others about it while I was walking Babette at the dog park, they also denied the affair. They said it never happened, and I shouldn't sully Eric's memory by voicing these baseless accusations and launching these rumors. Which is when I decided that my neighbors had apparently conspired to protect the identity of Eric's mistress, and I couldn't trust a single one of them."

"So how did you find out that it was Norma?"

"I actually overheard Mae and Julio talking about it the other day. They were in the backyard and hadn't seen me since I was taking in some sun. They mentioned Eric and Norma Parkman and said that Norma was at it again. This time with an even younger lover. So that's how I found out. I confronted Norma, and the rest of the story you know."

"Is that why you keep picking the Wests' cherries?"

"Wouldn't you? They're the ones who decided to protect Norma and lie to me. And besides, I never pick any cherries from their tree. I simply pick up the ones that fall into my backyard. At first, I handed them all back to them, but then once I found out about Eric's affair and how the Wests lied to me, I thought to hell with them. After I overheard them talking about Norma the other day, I baked a cherry cake, and we ate it on the deck, right under Mae's nose."

"But why didn't you tell us all of this before?" asked Odelia.

Holly shrugged. "I'm not proud of this feud I've got going on with my neighbors. And I didn't want to make things worse by telling you all about it. I knew you'd ask them a lot of questions and stir things up, and I'm already having a very hard time living here, with Mae and Julio going nuts over their cherry tree and Mark Cooper giving me a hard time over his precious parking spot. I just figured I'd leave all of that out since I didn't think it was relevant."

"Nobody seems to think Eric's affair was relevant, Max," said Dooley. "Not Holly and not Babette. But why do you think it's relevant?"

"Because that affair led to this feud Holly is having with her neighbors, and somehow I have a feeling it might have a bearing on the case." I didn't know how, though. But when I'm in the middle of a case, I'm like a dog with a bone: I can't stop digging!

"Do you think Eric's affair is connected with the death of that man?" asked Holly now.

"I'm not sure," Chase confessed. "But in a case like this, it's important that we follow every lead, wherever it might take us."

"Even if it unravels a lot of secrets nobody wants to be confronted with?"

"Even if it will force Norma Parkman to come clean to her husband," said Chase. "Or your neighbors to confront their enmity toward you."

"It has been very hard these last couple of years," Holly confessed.

"We talked to Chris Goldsworthy," said Odelia. "He says he's been trying to buy your house?"

Holly barked a humorless laugh. "I just wish these people would leave me alone. Why would I want to sell my house? I may not like my neighbors very much, but I'm perfectly happy with the house and the location. And besides, he's been trying to lowball me, offering a price that is well under the market value for the place. At first, I thought he was joking, but it turned out he was for real. Like my other neighbors, he seems to think I'm stupid." A touch of iron had entered her voice. "But I can assure you that I'm not. It's possible that I will sell, especially after everything that's happened, but the last person in the world I would sell to is Chris, or anyone else in this neighborhood for that matter."

CHAPTER 19

*W*e had made a promise to Babette, and we planned to keep it. So that evening, Dooley, Brutus, Harriet, and I walked along Russell Street on our way to Holly Mitchell's house to make sure it could be declared ghost-free. On our way there, we passed by the butcher shop and saw a makeup-free Norma Parkman serving a customer. Her eyes were red, and she had obviously been crying.

"I have the impression that Norma told her husband about the affair," said Dooley.

"What affair?" asked Harriet.

And so we told her and Brutus all about the affair that had gone on between Holly's husband and the butcher's wife four years ago.

"And all this happened right under the noses of Holly's neighbors, and they never said a word?"

"Never said a word," I confirmed.

"No wonder Holly is angry with them."

We had arrived at the house, so we snuck around the back and stared up at the place. All was dark, as expected, and I wondered how we were going to get inside. But then I remembered the pet door, and hoped it wouldn't be locked. Moments later, we were standing in the kitchen. As we paused for a moment to get our bearings, I have to say I found the house eerily quiet. Not all that pleasant to be in!

"We should have stayed home," Brutus complained. "To think we could be snuggling on the couch right now, settling in for a nice long evening."

"It's only one night, twinkle toes," said Harriet. "And if this ghost doesn't show up, which I'm sure he won't since ghosts don't exist, we'll be able to tell Babette that the coast is clear, and the family can return without any problem."

"But what if this ghost does show up?" asked Dooley. "Babette said that people who die suddenly and feel like they died too soon tend to linger and harass the living until they decide to move along."

"Ghosts don't exist, Dooley," Harriet repeated.

"Not even bonobo ghosts?" he asked in a small voice.

She stared at him in wonder. "I'm not even going to ask."

For a moment we debated where to set up our 'base of operations.' Harriet and Brutus thought we should be in the kitchen since, if there was a ghost, that's where he would be. But Dooley and I put our paw down on that option. Even though I don't believe in ghosts, I still didn't want to take any chances of being caught with our collars down, so to speak. So it was decided: we would set up in the living room with the kitchen door open, so we would be immediately alerted if the ghost decided to show up.

Before long, we had settled on the couch, keeping our eyes peeled.

"Is it true that ghosts are luminescent, Max?" asked Dooley. "I mean, do they glow in the dark?"

"I'm not an expert on ghosts, Dooley," I pointed out. "So I wouldn't know what they look like."

"I wonder how a man can suddenly turn into a bonobo, though. I mean, he's been human all his life, but now that he's dead, his ghost looks like a chimpanzee? That doesn't make any sense."

"It doesn't, because that's not what happens," Brutus said.

"It's not?"

"Of course not. And now shut up, will you? We're all trying to concentrate here."

He was right. This ghost-hunting was serious business, so we needed to focus. Unfortunately, I was focusing so hard that very soon I fell asleep. In my defense, it had been a long day, and I probably would have slept all night if not for the sudden sound of breaking glass that woke me up.

"It's the ghost!" Dooley cried. "He's here, Max!"

And quite possibly, he was right. Through the kitchen door, two dark figures now entered the house, looked left and right, before joining us in the living room.

"They're not luminescent," Dooley pointed out. "So at least that's one good thing. And they don't look like bonobos either. So that's also good. But they're still ghosts, Max, and they might harm us if we don't hide right now!"

And to show us how it was done, he hopped down from the couch and disappeared underneath.

"Maybe Dooley is right," Harriet said. She sounded a little shaky, I thought. "Maybe we should hide from these... ghosts!"

"They're not ghosts," Brutus insisted.

"How do you know?"

"Because ghosts don't have to break a window to get in!"

An excellent point, I had to admit. At least the ghosts I've heard about can simply move through walls and windows without having to resort to breaking them down. Or maybe these were beginning ghosts who hadn't gotten the hang of things yet. But when I looked a little closer, I saw that they had grabbed the large TV set and were trying to hoist it out of the room.

"These aren't ghosts," I finally concluded. "They're burglars!"

Dooley now emerged from under the couch. "Are you sure?"

"Of course! Look, they're stealing the television!"

And since we're basically not in favor of people who can't distinguish between mine and thine, we decided to spring into action. But before we could, suddenly bright lights shone in through the window, and loud voices could be heard declaring, "Put down that television right now and come out with your hands up!"

It was certainly a compelling statement, but even though personally I would have been inclined to follow these very detailed instructions, the two burglars weren't convinced. Instead, they redoubled their efforts to abscond with the television set, which was of the large and flatscreen variety, and hurried out through the kitchen door. And as we followed in their wake, still hopeful that we might prove instrumental in safeguarding Holly's property, more bright lights lit up the scene, and before long, both men were on the ground eating dirt, with some burly characters sitting on top of them.

"We've got them!" one of these burly characters declared.

"Call the cops!" another one suggested.

"I think you were right, Max," said Dooley now as he studied the men. "They're not ghosts. They're not even bonobos! They're just a couple of thieves."

It was a disappointment, of course. When you fully expect to run into a pair of bonobo ghosts and instead you meet a couple of common crooks, it's safe to say you will experience a certain letdown. Then again, I now wondered who these brave people could be who had so valiantly guarded Holly's property. Imagine my surprise when I discovered one of them was, in fact, Chris Goldsworthy.

"Who are these people, Max?" asked Brutus.

"Neighborhood watch," I said. "That one over there is the leader of the watch, and if I'm not mistaken the other fellow just might be Julio West. The one from the cherry tree?"

"Oh, right, the cherry tree," said Brutus as he glanced in the direction of said tree. And to show us that he thought this tree and all of its produce were rightfully his, Mr. West had now walked up to that tree and was plucking cherries, putting them into his mouth and spitting out the pits.

Mr. Goldsworthy, still straddling one of the burglars, now took out his phone to call the police. Unfortunately, before he could put the device to his ear, there was another altercation. This time, two older ladies descended upon the scene, shouting, "Put down your weapons—you're all under arrest!"

They were, of course, Gran and her friend Scarlett Canyon, and they were both armed to the teeth. Gran was clutching pepper spray in her hand and didn't look afraid to use it, and Scarlett held a stun gun in her hand, aiming it straight at Mr. West, who now stood frozen, his hands in the air.

"We're the watch!" said Chris Goldsworthy.

"Nonsense—we're the watch!" said Gran.

"No, but this is our turf," said Chris. "This is where we patrol."

"Yeah, and we just caught these here burglars," Julio West added.

"A likely story," Gran growled. "From where I'm standing, you're all burglars! And you're all going to rot in jail for the rest of your miserable lives!"

"You're making a big mistake, lady," said Chris, trying to get up from his uncomfortable position.

"Don't move!" Gran yelled and motioned with the pepper spray. "I'm not afraid to use this, you know."

"We're the one and only Hampton Cove neighborhood watch," Scarlett declared with satisfaction, "and you're all under arrest. And that goes for you too, pretty boy."

"Would you say he's pretty?" asked Gran as she studied Chris Goldsworthy's handsome face.

"For a criminal, he's very attractive," said Scarlett. She sighed. "I just hope they won't hurt him too much in prison. You know what they do with pretty boys in jail."

"Oh, for crying out loud!" Chris said.

Moments later, a police siren could be heard, and before long, we were joined by two members of Hampton Cove PD's finest. They seemed a little surprised when they found no less than four men being held at gunpoint by two elderly ladies. Though gunpoint was perhaps not the correct word, since neither of them actually held a gun.

"I'm not a crook!" Chris declared heatedly. "I'm the leader of the neighborhood watch!"

"Of course you are," said one of the arresting officers and proceeded to read the man his rights. A second police car had arrived, and before long, all four men were arrested and carted off to the precinct for processing and the lockup.

Gran and Scarlett exchanged high fives for a job well done and received compliments from the officers on the scene. It must have been a heady experience since mostly they're the ones being placed under arrest after they've been up to another one of their stunts. This time they had done a good job. Though when I told Gran that two of the men had been members of the local neighborhood watch, she seemed disappointed.

"It's sad when people who should be on the right side of

the law go astray, Max," she confessed. "Hopefully, they'll see the error of their ways after a night in the lockup and will tell the judge in the morning they'll never do it again. With a good lawyer, I'm sure their sentences will be greatly reduced."

"But... they weren't breaking into Holly's house," I said. "They were actually the ones who stopped the actual burglars from getting away with her television." I pointed to the flatscreen which was still lying on the lawn. "If not for Chris Goldsworthy and Julio West, these men would probably have emptied out the whole house."

"Oh, so you know these people, do you?" asked Gran.

"Of course. Chris Goldsworthy runs the local neighborhood watch."

She patted my head. "Maxie, Maxie, you shouldn't be so trusting, my friend. When you're my age, you'll start to see through these obvious lies. The four of them were in it together, anyone can see that. This so-called watch was on the lookout while the burglars did their thing. Then when the loot was sold with the assistance of a fence, the money was to be divided between them." She heaved a deep sigh. "Good thing we showed up." Then she seemed to realize something. "But what were you doing here?"

"Looking for a ghost," Dooley explained. "Babette thought that the ghost of the dead man would show up and haunt the place. But all we saw were those two crooks and then the neighborhood watch people arresting them. And then you showed up and arrested all of them."

Gran gave him a kindly smile. "And a good thing we did!"

"But Gran!" I said.

She shut me up with a single look. "Crime doesn't pay, Max. I think we've established that once again here tonight. Now, do you want to stay here looking for this non-existent ghost, or do you want to ride with the watch?"

And since the last thing we wanted was to wait for some ghost to show up, we decided to take her up on her offer. I just hoped she wouldn't arrest more neighborhood watch members. Somehow, I had a feeling Chris Goldsworthy hadn't enjoyed the experience, and neither had Julio West.

CHAPTER 20

*R*iding with the watch is always a fun proposition, and since both Gran and Scarlett were in an exceptionally good mood after having caught no less than four crooks—at least in their minds—it was even more fun than usual. The two ladies were keen to celebrate their win, but first, they wanted to complete their shift, in the hopes of ridding Hampton Cove of even more criminals. They hadn't forgotten about the homeless people occupying our local park, and had been working on a possible solution. If we had hoped to hop out to enjoy some time participating in our favorite activities at cat choir, we were sorely mistaken, for Gran's keen eyes had spotted something untoward.

"Will you look at that," she said. She had parked her car on the side of the road and pointed a bony finger to a van that had halted not fifty yards in front of us. From the back of the van, a group of men emerged, all looking very much the worse for wear.

"More homeless people," asked Scarlett.

"But what are they doing in that van?"

We watched as more vans pulled up, and more homeless people were escorted out. It was a curious sight, to be sure, as all of the men received a plastic bag and an envelope from the drivers of the vans. Then, after they had been pointed to the park, the drivers got into their vans and took off again.

"I don't understand," Brutus confessed.

"I think I know what's going on," I said. "Someone is paying these drivers to ferry these people in and drop them off here. That envelope is probably a small sum of money for their troubles, and those plastic bags are filled with some stuff they might need when sleeping rough like this."

"They're called swag bags, Max," Harriet informed me. "It's probably some creams and lotions and deodorant and maybe a nice expensive watch."

"This isn't the Oscars, Harriet," I pointed out, "and these people aren't celebrities."

"I think we better investigate," Gran announced. She turned back to us. "Get out there and find out what's going on. We'll stay here and monitor the situation, just in case more of these vans show up."

Scarlett held up her phone. "I snapped a couple of shots. I'm sure the police will be interested to know who those vans belong to."

"Good thinking, honey," said Gran. "I'll clue in Alec." And so she took out her own phone to call her son while the four of us stepped out of the car. We had received our instructions, and now it was go time!

Before long, we had found the group, who had joined the others who had taken over the park these past couple of weeks. They looked around a little uncertainly, as one does when arriving at a new destination, but before long, the old guard had informed the new guard about sleeping arrangements, and they all settled in. We snuck up to one of the benches where two bums sat sharing a bottle of liquor. One had been there for a while, and the other one was new, but they got along famously.

"Oh, this is a fine little town," said the old-timer. "Mighty fine. You've got your hospitable people who don't mind sharing their riches, and you've got your nice beach down there, your shopping mall at walking distance, a nice strip mall. All in all, a great place to live."

"I was doing fine in New York," the newcomer revealed. "Until all of a sudden, this guy shows up telling me I could be doing so much better in the Hamptons. But when I told him there's not much going on in the Hamptons, he said that's where I was wrong, since there was this lively community here, and now I can see he wasn't mistaken."

"Same thing here," said the old-timer. "Where were you located?"

"Brooklyn," said the other man.

"Oh, isn't that a coincidence! I was in Brooklyn too. Rapture Park, first bench from the left."

"I was on Parker Street. And before that on Meadows Lane."

"I'm glad you've decided to join us, brother."

Harriet, who had taken a sniff from one of the bags, said, "You were right, Max. It's not a swag bag. As far as I can tell, it's filled with food, but not the kind I would like to dig my teeth into. I smell mostly candy and canned food."

"And the envelope is filled with cash," said Brutus, who had taken a quick peek as one of the men got busy checking the contents of his little haul.

"They seem like nice additions to our local community, Max," Dooley said.

"I'm not sure everyone will agree with that assessment, Dooley," I said. "The kind of people a town likes to see are the ones who get a paying job, contribute to the local economy, pay their taxes, rent or buy." I had the impression these people weren't going to do any of that. Then again, I could be mistaken, of course. Maybe they would prove to be a real boon to our town and become pillars of society. As things stood, though, I really wondered who this person could be that had been recruiting these people to leave their bench in Brooklyn to relocate to a bench in Hampton Cove. And I had a feeling Uncle Alec would be most interested as well. Even though they weren't disturbing the peace, they were turning our lovely park into a campsite, which it presumably hadn't been designed for.

And so we sneaked back out of the park and returned to where Gran was waiting. We informed her about the conversation we had overheard, and she told us she had already talked to her son, and the police chief was sending a couple of officers to talk to the men and find out what was going on.

"Someone is ferrying in homeless people," she concluded. "But who? And why?"

"Must be this man who recruited them in Brooklyn," I said.

"You didn't get a name, did you?" asked Gran.

I shook my head. "I'll bet he's not the person who's organizing all of this, though. The recruiter is probably being paid just like the drivers are. The organizer is probably someone the homeless people haven't seen. Someone who operates behind the scenes."

"The watch will catch him," said Gran firmly. "And then we'll send him where we put those other crooks."

"But why, Gran?" asked Dooley. "He's not breaking any laws, is he? After all, he's simply providing transport and offering these people money and food. If anything, this man is a hero. He should be rewarded, not punished."

Gran smiled and patted Dooley on the cheek. "This man

isn't a hero, honey. I'm pretty sure he's not doing this out of the goodness of his own heart but for some more nefarious reason."

"But what?"

"That," she said, "is something we'll have to figure out."

CHAPTER 21

Since there didn't seem to be a lot more we could do, the four of us decided to join cat choir while Gran and Scarlett returned home to enjoy some much-needed rest. When we arrived at our designated spot, we found, however, that not only had the playground been taken over by the homeless crowd, but there was no trace of our friends.

"Where is cat choir?" asked Harriet, much dismayed. Cat choir is by way of being her raison d'être, after all. She enjoys the privilege of being its star soprano and doesn't like to waste even a single night not giving us the benefit of her God-given talent.

"Maybe they finished already?" Brutus suggested.

"Or maybe they relocated?" I said.

But Dooley had a different idea. "Oh, my God, you guys!" he cried. "They're eating Shanille!" He was pointing to a small group of homeless people who were roasting something over a slow fire. It was a small animal with the exact size and shape of a cat.

We all stared at the troubling scene with horror written all over our faces.

"This can't be happening," said Harriet. "They've killed our choir conductor, and they're going to eat her!"

"Over my dead body," Brutus growled, and before we could stop him, he was running over to the small gathering, gaining speed as he progressed. Finally, he approached them at maximum velocity, and as he launched himself into the air, he hit the object roasting over the fire and dislodged it from its position. Both Brutus and the lifeless object rolled over the ground until they both came to a full stop against a nearby tree. Then Brutus stood over the remains of our conductor, crying bitter tears and imploring her to "Come back to us, Shanille! Don't die!"

But as far as I could tell, it was already too late.

We all joined our friend, much to the astonishment of the homeless folks who had been deprived of their meal, and folded our paws in prayer.

"She was a wonderful conductor," I said.

"The very best," Brutus added.

"She will be missed," Dooley sniffled.

"Oh, what am I going to do without my best frenemy!" Harriet cried, raising her paws heavenward and shaking them disconsolately.

"What are you guys doing?" suddenly a voice rang out behind us.

We looked up and, to our surprise, the voice belonged to none other than... Shanille!

"But... I thought you were dead," said Brutus, looking from the lifeless object at our feet to Shanille.

"Dead? Why would I be dead?" asked Shanille. She glanced down at the homeless people's former meal. "And why are you crying over a dead rat?"

"A rat?" asked Harriet, recoiling a little. "We thought that was you!"

Shanille laughed, but I could tell her heart wasn't in it. "I'm glad you finally decided to show up," she said. "You missed the most shambolic cat choir rehearsal in history. When we arrived here, the place was crawling with these men who all look a little worse for wear. And before long, they started hunting us. No idea why. They almost grabbed Buster, but we managed to get him out of their clutches. But then they got Kingman and dragged him over there, to that fire. It was Clarice who led the first assault and the second, but it was only when we attacked them for the third time that we managed to get him back safe and sound." She shook her head. "I guess when they realized they wouldn't have cat on the menu tonight, they decided to go for a nice juicy rat instead."

"Max, watch out!" suddenly Dooley cried. Just in time, I saw that one of the men pounced at me, clearly with the intention of capturing me.

"A nice fat one, Bernie!" he cried as he made a grab for me.

"Oh yeah, get that one, Jackie," said his mate. "Lots of meat on those bones!"

"Run, Max!" Harriet yelled. "Run like the wind."

I don't know about the wind, but I did run, and pretty speedily too! In fact, we all ran, and when we finally arrived on the other side of the park, the section that gives out onto the beach, we saw that the rest of cat choir was gathered there, looking out across the beach where several fires were burning bright.

"What's going on?" I asked, slightly out of breath after our great escape.

"Not sure," said Kingman, who was among those present. "Looks like they're roasting something."

"Is anyone missing?" asked Shanille.

We all shivered as the inference was clear. If these people had tried to grab Buster, Kingman, and now me, maybe they had succeeded and were roasting some of our friends!

"Fish," Clarice announced, suddenly showing up next to me. "They're not roasting cats, if that's what you think. They managed to catch themselves some fish, and now they're going to eat them."

I think we all breathed a sigh of relief. But it was still evident that our once pleasant little town suddenly wasn't so pleasant anymore.

It was probably safe to say that none of us were in the mood to sing, so the rehearsal was canceled. Even Harriet decided that now was not the time to launch into her personal rendition of a power ballad. Besides, we didn't want to attract attention to ourselves and potentially become targets.

"Looks like the food in those plastic bags didn't last long," said Dooley as we watched the eerie scene.

"Or that money," Brutus supplied.

We told the others about the vans and the people being ferried in, and they all agreed that a gang of human traffickers was active in our town for reasons that were unclear. "Usually, you have to pay these people to take you someplace," said Shanille. "But in this case, it's them who pay. It's odd."

"Do you think it's connected to the murder of Antoine O'Neil, Max?" asked Dooley. "After all, he was also one of these people."

"It's possible," I allowed. "Though right now, I can't see the connection yet."

"You will," Brutus said, clapping me on the shoulder, a little more forcefully than I would have liked. "Just put that big brain of yours to good use, Maxie baby, and you'll figure it out."

"Make haste, Max," Shanille implored. "Because I don't want to be eaten!"

CHAPTER 22

$\mathcal{W}$e made it home in one piece and found our humans in bed, asleep by the time we got there. They, at least, seemed unconcerned by the stunning events that had taken place. We had agreed with the other cat choir members to travel in packs for the time being so that if we were attacked, we would be able to defend ourselves. And since I guess we were all feeling spooked, we decided to stick together even inside our own home.

So when Odelia and Chase woke up the next morning, they were surprised to find not two but four cats resting peacefully at the foot of the bed. I could feel them stir, but since I was just dreaming of a nice bowl of kibble, filled to the brim, I didn't immediately wake up. It actually took me a while to achieve full wakefulness, and when I did, I discovered that Dooley was already telling Odelia all about what happened. The burglars, the watch business, the vans ferrying in homeless people straight from Brooklyn, and the men trying to catch us so they could roast us over a nice fire and fill their tummies.

Odelia was as shocked as we had been, and she quickly

informed her husband. A resolute look came over Chase's face, and he promised to get to the bottom of this business with the homeless people, which had grown to the proportions of a minor crisis at this point. Just then, his phone chimed, and when he picked it up from the nightstand, he announced, "Your uncle," and answered the call.

It turned out that Uncle Alec had been summoned to the Mayor's office, and so had Chase and Odelia. And since Odelia didn't want us to feel left out, she extended an invitation to join them. Which is why half an hour later, we all found ourselves in the Mayor's office, Charlene Butterwick herself seated behind her desk, and Uncle Alec, Chase, and Odelia in front of her. Also present were Gran and Scarlett. Charlene had folded her hands on top of her desk and calmly surveyed the faces in front of her. "This town is facing a major crisis," she announced. "And I think it's time we acted. I have received several complaints in the past couple of days about women being harassed on the street, others being robbed, phones stolen, purses snatched. There's been a spate of burglaries, with mostly televisions being stolen, valuables and cash taken. And people are complaining about drug addicts shooting up on the street in front of their kids and generally creating a dangerous and unpleasant atmosphere." She turned to her fiancé. "What can you tell us about the arrests that were made last night?"

"Well, they were part of the same homeless community, alright," said Uncle Alec. "They said they had received a tip-off that there was untold riches to be found at the house of Holly Mitchell. Luckily for Mrs. Mitchell, they were apprehended by two members of the local watch committee, Christopher Goldsworthy and Julio West, who unfortunately ran afoul of a second neighborhood watch, this one comprised of my mother and Scarlett." He directed a scathing look at his mom, who took it in stride.

"How was I supposed to know they were watch members?"

"They specifically told you they belonged to the watch, Ma."

"Why believe them? Anyone can say they're part of a neighborhood watch. They sure looked suspicious enough to me."

"But also very handsome," said Scarlett. "Especially that Christopher Goldsworthy."

"Too handsome, if you ask me," Gran grunted. "Only criminals can look that handsome." She turned to her son. "Are you sure they're not both gangsters?"

"No, Ma! Christopher Goldsworthy is a lawyer, and Julio West works for the LIRR. They're both upstanding citizens who formed a neighborhood watch a couple of months ago and were instrumental in the capture of the burglars last night."

"We caught those burglars!" said Gran.

"After the other watch caught them!"

"Okay, enough about that," said Charlene, holding up her hands. "Please don't go around arresting other watch members," she told Gran. "Though it is good that those two crooks were arrested, of course. Did they say who told them this 'untold riches' story?"

"Antoine O'Neil," said the Chief. "Who got it from some unknown woman. But don't worry, we'll discover her identity soon enough."

"Okay, now about those human traffickers. What's their game? Why Hampton Cove? And why pay these people money to come here? I don't understand."

"Me neither," Uncle Alec admitted. "We checked the license plates of the vans that were seen bringing these people in last night." He directed an appreciative nod to Scarlett for taking the pictures, who responded in kind. "And they're all registered in New York. So Chase here will liaise with the NYPD to interview these people and find out what's going on."

"They're trying to capture our cats," said Odelia. "Last night, they tried to grab Max." Her voice had taken on a quivery note, and I could tell that she was shaken to the core. "Something needs to be done, Charlene. My cats are afraid to walk the street at night. They're afraid to come near the park."

"My God," said Charlene. "This is a nightmare. There are simply too many of them, and things are starting to get completely out of hand."

"Can't you arrest these people?" asked Scarlett. "Take them off the street?"

"We can arrest them when they're breaking the law," said Uncle Alec. "When they're dealing drugs or using illegal substances or engaging in purse-snatching or breaking into people's homes. But the penalties are mild for these offenses, and before long, they're out on the street again."

"Isn't there a law against camping out in the park?" asked Odelia.

"Unfortunately not. Unless you put up some kind of structure—a tent, let's say—there's no law against sleeping outside. Some towns and cities have an ordinance that closes down the parks at night, but we never had that since we have never been faced with this kind of problem before."

"Maybe you should start providing shelter," Uncle Alec suggested.

"Maybe we should," Charlene agreed. "I've called a special meeting of the council to discuss the problem. And I hope we'll find a solution soon because this is really getting out of control. First and foremost, though, we need to stem the flow and make sure these people smugglers, or whatever you want to call them, are stopped. Someone is bringing these people to Hampton Cove, and we need to find out who and hold them accountable somehow."

"We're on it," said Uncle Alec curtly.

"And please, stop them from trying to eat our cats," said Charlene. "Or our dogs, for that matter."

CHAPTER 23

*a*s we walked out of Town Hall, we saw that the two men who had been arrested last night had been released. Chris Goldsworthy and Julio West looked a little soiled, and their faces weren't as smoothly shaven as they had been before, but otherwise, they were fine. I watched as they walked along and saw that they took a seat on one of the benches placed in the little square in front of Town Hall. Trees provide shade and a fountain provides some cooling, making it a popular spot for both locals and tourists. And since I'm a very curious kitty, I decided to sneak up on the watch members and listen in on their conversation.

Joining me were my friends, who were still greatly impressed by the events of last night and had no intention of allowing me to wander off on my own. This time, the four musketeers would stay together at all costs.

"We should press charges," Chris was saying as he patted his hair to ascertain whether it was still bouffant. "They can't do this to us, you know. Arrest us like that. We didn't do anything wrong."

"The woman is the Chief's mother," Julio pointed out. "So

I think it's safe to say she's beyond legal consequences. And I guess that cop had a point when he said we should have registered the watch with them."

"What nonsense. All we did was arrest two criminals, and instead, we're the ones being thrown in jail? It's outrageous. An absolute disgrace."

"We have to do things by the book, Chris. We can't afford any more of these snafus. Especially considering..." He glanced left and right, making sure he wasn't overheard, then lowered his voice. "Especially considering our little project."

"Yeah, I guess you're right. The project is more important than our personal honor. And they did apologize."

"So how is it going?" asked Julio, digging into his pockets and retrieving a pack of cigarettes and a lighter.

"Oh, fine, fine," said Chris. "Last night, they brought in another couple of dozen of those poor souls."

"Is it enough, you think?"

"Not by a mile. Have you read anything in the paper yet? Seen anything on the news? As long as the authorities think they can simply ignore the problem, that means we haven't done our jobs."

Julio had lit his cigarette and took a deep drag. "House prices are still the same," he said. "So I guess you're right. Things haven't gone far enough yet. Though it'll probably be a couple of months before we really see any change."

"At the very least. These things take time. First, we need to hit the local papers, then the national ones. By that time, maybe people will start to realize that Hampton Cove isn't the lovely little town they always thought it was."

"A hellhole," said Julio acerbically and grinned a rat-like grin.

"That's exactly what we need to establish: Hampton Cove as a hellhole. Then, and only then, will property prices finally take a nosedive, and that's when we'll make a killing, buddy."

"Oh, I can't wait," said Julio. "The sooner the better, if I'm honest. If I have to stay in that job for even another week, I'll go nuts."

"Same here," Chris agreed. "Though we'll just have to hang in there. Not for a week, but for months, possibly up to a year."

"I know. And I can do it as long as I know that it will be worth the sacrifice."

"It will be worth it, trust me. The moment we've snapped up all the pieces of real estate we've got our eye on, we'll get rid of the bums, the market will recover, and we'll be on velvet. Millionaires!"

"Millionaires," Julio murmured with an ecstatic look on his face.

"And what do we have here?" asked Chris. He gestured to Odelia, Chase, Uncle Alec, Gran, and Scarlett walking out of Town Hall and standing on the steps for a moment to discuss the meeting that had just taken place. "The chief of police, his niece, that detective, and those two horrible old women."

"Looks like things are finally heating up," said Julio, well pleased.

And since I figured we'd heard enough, we decided to trip over to where our humans stood and tell them all about the dastardly plans of Mr. Goldsworthy and Mr. West. Odelia listened attentively, then fastened her eyes on the duo. Moments later, she was apprising the rest of the select company of the same, and as we watched on, both the Chief and Chase legged it over to the bench and arrested the two men on the spot. We could hear their loud lament all the way to where we were standing.

Turns out the mystery of the influx of homeless people wasn't such a big mystery after all. Chris and Julio had read somewhere that the value of real estate in cities with a large homeless population drops precipitously. And over a beer, they had decided to create such a situation in their own home town as well. They figured they needed to reach a 'critical mass' of a certain number of people living rough on the streets and causing an uproar in the local community, and soon word would spread and tourists would start to shun our town and stay away. Property prices would fall, and they would be able to snap up a couple of pieces of prime real estate at bargain-bottom prices. Then, once the problem was remedied, the prices would shoot up again, and they could unload their properties at a profit. It sounded like a great plan, only they hadn't accounted for the impact a couple of hundred people living on the streets of our town would have on everything from the local economy to the livability.

All in all, it seemed like an ill-conceived idea, and if Uncle Alec had his wish, the two men would pay dearly for their initiative.

We were present when Chris Goldsworthy was being interviewed by Chase and Odelia, and it wasn't long before the man sang like the proverbial canary.

"Okay, I shouldn't have done it," he admitted. "But then the idea was too good to ignore. And what are a couple of homeless? Someone should take care of them, right? So why not us?" He gave them his most pious expression, but they weren't fooled.

"Don't act like a great humanitarian," Chase said. "The only reason you did this was to make money."

"What's wrong with making money? We're an entrepreneurial society."

"You were trying to make money on the back of those people you ferried in," said Chase, tapping his finger on the table and leaning forward. "Not to mention the havoc you wreaked on your own town. And you're supposed to be the leader of a neighborhood watch! Don't you have any shame?"

"Obviously not," Brutus commented.

Harriet sighed. "At least we won't get eaten now."

"I wouldn't be so sure," said Brutus. "Now that these people are here, I don't see how they'll get them to leave again."

The idea had occurred to Chase, so he now asked, "How were you planning on making them leave?"

"Oh, we would have thought of something," said Chris airily. "Offer them money to move to the next town, maybe. I hadn't thought it through."

"Obviously you hadn't," said Chase acerbically. "Okay, something else. You decided to manipulate property prices. We also know that you wanted to buy the house next door. So did you pay Antoine O'Neil and Toby Grave to break into the house of your neighbor, Holly Mitchell?"

"What? Of course not! I would never do a thing like that."

"Forgive me if I don't believe you, Chris. From where I'm sitting, this looks exactly like the kind of stunt you would pull. Pay two of your protégés to break into Mrs. Mitchell's house, scare the living daylights out of her, and force her to sell."

"But I didn't! I don't even know these people!"

Harriet turned to me. "I thought you said a woman paid Antoine to break in?"

"It's possible that Antoine lied," I told her. "And that it was this guy instead."

"We know someone paid Grave and O'Neil to break into that house," Chase continued his interrogation of his suspect. "And we also know you paid them to come to Hampton Cove. So better come clean now, Chris. Cause if we find out later that you've lied to us..."

"I'm not lying. I never came near those people." He wrinkled up his nose. "I mean, can you imagine me associating with that crowd? No way, detective."

Chase gave him a look of disgust. "You know what? You make me sick."

"Let me tell you what I think happened," said Odelia. "You paid Antoine O'Neil to break into your neighbor's house. You knew the exact time he would be there, since you had arranged to meet him. What did you do? Spy on Holly? Make sure she was out and then contact your little friend?"

Chris watched her with wide-eyed astonishment. "You're crazy!"

"Antoine showed up as arranged, and so did you. But when you arrived, instead of paying him what you had promised, you shot him point-blank."

"No!"

"A break-in would have scared Holly, but you weren't one hundred percent sure it would have made her pack up and leave. But a murder? In her own home? Now that might do the trick. And since you knew that everything would point to Antoine's friend Toby Grave, you figured it was a risk-free plan. And you were right. We did arrest Toby Grave. He denied everything, of course, but that was to be expected. And who would believe the word of a bum and a drug addict? So you knew he would probably go down for the murder of his friend, Holly Mitchell would move out as quickly as she could, happy to accept any offer on the house you were prepared to make, preferably as low as possible, and you would finally get what you always wanted. How am I doing so far, Chris?"

"Lousy! Okay, so I wanted her out of there, that's true. But I wasn't going to commit murder! I mean, I may be a lot of things, but I'm not a murderer! I'm the leader of the neighborhood watch!"

"Yeah, yeah," said Chase, "we've heard that a million times by now. The leader of the watch who decided to turn his own town into a shantytown." He got up and knocked on the

149

door of the interview room. An officer showed up, and Chase said, "Get this man out of my sight before I throw up."

"I didn't do this!" Chris insisted as he was being led away. "I don't even own a gun. You're making a big mistake, Detective Kingsley! A very big mistake! I didn't kill that man, I swear!"

But Chase paid him no mind. He knew he had caught Antoine O'Neil's killer and also the man who had brought trouble to the detective's adopted town. In his mind, he had solved two cases in one go. And as he and Odelia shared a look of relief, I had to confess Odelia had made a compelling case against Mr. Goldsworthy.

Dooley turned to me. "So, about that ghost, Max."

"Oh, not again with the ghost!" Harriet cried.

"Well, that ghost is still out there," Dooley argued. "So we still need to catch it. Are we going back out there tonight, Max? Make sure Holly's house is ghost-free? After all, we promised Babette."

"There was no ghost, remember?" asked Brutus.

"Maybe there was," Dooley said, "but it was scared off by those two burglars. If they hadn't shown up, I'm sure we would have seen the ghost. So we have to go back and catch it and talk to it, convince the ghost to leave."

"And how are we supposed to do that?" asked Harriet with an eye roll.

"Simple. We talk to it and explain to the ghost of Antoine O'Neil who his killer was and why it all happened. And that Chris Goldsworthy is going to jail for the murder. That way, Antoine's ghost can find peace and will move on." He gave me a pleading look. "Please, Max. Otherwise, Holly and her kids will never be able to return to the house, and neither will Babette. We have to do this—we promised."

Finally, I relented. "Oh, all right."

"Maybe it's not such a bad idea," Brutus said, much to my

surprise. "If this ghost really lingers in that house..." He shrugged. "I mean, what harm can it do to take another look, right?"

"Fine," said Harriet. "It's not as if we can go to cat choir tonight."

Her words reminded us all that this predicament of being eaten still hung over our heads. It's not a nice feeling, I can tell you, that there are actually people out there who wouldn't mind bashing your head in and then grilling your mortal remains. Not a nice feeling at all!

And so, we agreed we would take another whack at this ghost-hunting business. If no ghost showed up, so much the better. And if it did? Maybe we could follow Dooley's script and persuade it to move right along.

Holly would thank us, and so would Babette. And after all the trouble Hampton Cove had found itself in lately, spreading a little sweetness and light was just what the doctor ordered, and something we certainly could provide.

CHAPTER 24

The night had come, and once again the four of us were present and accounted for in Holly's house, hoping to encounter a ghost. Though, in all honesty, I would like to say that I personally was hoping not to encounter a ghost. As far as I can tell, ghosts are fickle creatures, and you never know what to expect from them. Since they are, by design, disembodied beings, it's very hard to know what they will do next. They could attack you just as soon as embrace you. Truth be told, even though I had definitively posited that I did not believe in ghosts, when we sat there in that dark, quiet house, I was starting to experience my first doubts. As a non-believer, it's all very well and good to state your lack of faith in the existence of ghosts, but once you're at the scene, waiting to encounter such a creature, it's quite a different thing altogether!

"Good thing cat choir was canceled," Harriet said, breaking the eerie silence. "Otherwise, we wouldn't have been able to hold this stakeout."

"Yeah, good thing," Brutus confirmed.

"Actually, I would very much have preferred going to cat

choir than having to sit here and wait for a ghost," I confessed.

"We can't go to cat choir, Max," said Dooley. "People there will eat us. And even though I'm not sure about meeting a ghost, I still think it beats being eaten."

"Isn't that the truth?" Brutus grunted.

"I hope cat choir won't be canceled indefinitely," said Harriet. "What am I going to do with my enormous talent? How am I going to let it be known to the world that I can sing—that I can dance—that I'm a star!"

"I'm sure cat choir will return," Brutus said. "As soon as those cat eaters are gone, and the park is safe again, Shanille will call us all together and announce the great comeback of cat choir. And then you can sing your heart out, buttercup."

"I hope so," said Harriet. "I miss it already, and it's only been one night."

Charlene had announced her intention to call an emergency meeting of the town council to deal with this crisis head-on. Presumably, they would close down the park at night and make sure the police patrolled the area. A shelter would be organized where the homeless people currently holed up in the park could stay, and the organizers of the people smuggling operation would be dealt with to the fullest extent of the law. Chris Goldsworthy and Julio West would not get away with this. The point of contention at the moment was whether they were also guilty of the murder of Antoine O'Neil. Both men vehemently denied the charge, as, of course, they would, but even I wasn't fully convinced they were behind the murder. It definitely was in line with their interests, of course, especially Chris wanting to buy Holly's house at all costs—though preferably for as low a price as possible.

For now, the jury was still out on that particular charge, but they had both confessed to the scheme of ferrying in homeless people from all across the state to depress our local real estate market and make a killing in the process. Surrounding towns had offered to help bear the burden of the homeless persons' presence, and I was convinced that very soon now the crisis would be averted.

The fact still remained that until further notice, the park would remain closed at night, though for us cats, that didn't pose too much of a problem since that order only applied to people and not to pets or animals of any description. Maybe it was even better this way since no one would be present to interrupt our peaceful gatherings.

We had sat on that sofa for the better part of two hours, and the clock was pointing near one o'clock when suddenly something appeared to stir. We heard distinct noises coming from the kitchen, and as Brutus narrowed his eyes, he said under his breath, "You guys—someone is trying to break in!"

"Oh, not again!" said Harriet. "What's wrong with these people?"

"Apparently, Holly's house is very popular," I said.

"It's the ghost," Dooley said, sounding extremely excited. "This is it, you guys. The ghost has finally decided to show his face! Let's get ready!"

How one can possibly get ready to meet a ghost was beyond me, but we still dug our claws into that couch and got ready for any contingency.

All we could hear for the next couple of minutes was someone monkeying with the door lock, and judging from the cursing this person produced, they weren't successful in their attempts. It reminded me of Gran and Scarlett, who had, on occasion, also felt the need to break into places under the cover of darkness and generally not been very successful. Breaking into houses is an art and takes a very special set of skills. And even though you may have watched a few YouTube videos on the topic, that doesn't make you any more proficient than the common layman.

Finally, the attempts to pass the hurdle of the locked door proved successful, and the door swung open. The person now entering was wearing a hoodie, apparently the favored costume of the breaker-and-enterer, and for a moment just stood there. Then the burglar approached and joined us in the living room.

"It's not a ghost," Brutus announced. "Ghosts don't bother with messing with locks."

"I think it is a ghost," Dooley said. "It's the ghost of Antoine O'Neil, and he's simply repeating what he did two nights ago. That's what ghosts do, you know. They keep repeating the same behavior that got them killed, trying to come to terms with what happened. So this is definitely Antoine O'Neil's ghost, repeating his exact movements of the night. He broke into the kitchen, then moved into the living room to start his burglarious attempts to find the promised untold riches."

"I thought he was killed in the kitchen?" said Brutus.

"He'll soon return to the kitchen," Dooley said. "Just you wait and see. And then he will reenact the scene of his murder."

"I don't think so, Dooley," I said. "I think this is an actual person burgling Holly's house right now. And we have to think of something to stop them."

"I hear what you're saying, Max," said my friend. "But I don't agree. And I'm going to prove to you once and for all that this here is the ghost of Antoine O'Neil."

And before we could stop him, he suddenly launched himself off the couch and at the person, who still stood stock-still in the living room, clearly unsure how to proceed.

"Dooley, no!" I said.

But too late. Dooley was already moving at great speed toward the so-called ghost, eager to prove his point.

"I'm going to move right through him!" he announced. "Just you watch!"

And as we watched on, trepidation freezing us to our spots on the couch, instead of moving right through Antoine's ghost, Dooley bumped into him. And since humans prove pretty much an immovable object since they're that much bigger than us, our friend was repelled by the presence of the burglar and bumped back onto his tush.

"Ouch," he said, staring up at the person. "That's weird. He's pretty solid."

"That's because it's not a ghost but an actual person," I told him. "Now get back here before he catches you!"

"And eats you!" Harriet added.

"Probably one of those bums again," Brutus said. "Let's hope he didn't bring a portable grill so he can barbecue us!"

The person must not have even noticed Dooley, for he or she now moved in the direction of a large cabinet, flicked on a flashlight, and started rifling through its drawers. And when that didn't yield whatever they were looking for, next up was a tall kitchen cupboard. Before long, every possible piece of furniture in the house was being subjected to a thorough search.

"Your ghost is just a common burglar," Brutus told Dooley.

"Too bad," said Dooley. "Now the real ghost will be scared off again. Why can't they simply leave us alone? They keep interrupting our ghost hunt!"

"Look, if there really was a ghost," I said, "he wouldn't bother with any burglars. Ghosts don't care about the living all that much, as far as I'm aware. So burglar or not, if Antoine O'Neil was haunting this place, he would have shown himself by now. The fact that he hasn't means he's not a ghost."

"But he has to be a ghost!" Dooley insisted. "Every person who dies suddenly and doesn't understand why turns into a ghost. It's a law of nature."

"Don't tell me you got that from your Discovery Channel," Brutus scoffed. "For I think that's just a load of rubbish, Dooley. Like Max already pointed out, ghosts probably don't exist. And we should try and stop this burglar from robbing Holly blind."

"Brutus is right," said Harriet. "We can't let this person steal a lot of Holly's stuff. So what do you suggest, my braveheart?"

"Our home is just a quick trip through the backyard away," said Brutus. "One of us should go and fetch Odelia. That way she can cut off this 'ghost.'" And since none of us is faster than Brutus, we all stared at him until he finally relented. "All right, fine. I'll do it. Just make sure that burglar doesn't go anywhere, you hear? Because you know what humans are like. Once they're fast asleep, it's not easy to wake them up!"

"Use your words, Brutus," Dooley advised.

"Or use your claws," Harriet suggested.

"Or just jump on top of her head," I said. "She hates it when we do that."

Brutus grinned. "Maybe I'll do all of that at the same time. She's bound to wake up after that treatment. I just hope she won't strike back at me in anger!"

And with these words, our brave friend ventured out into that cold night to alert our humans that another burglary was in progress at Holly's place. Apparently, all the burglars in Hampton Cove were aware by now that Holly wasn't home and that some good stuff was to be gotten there!

And since Brutus had told us to make sure the burglar did

not escape, we decided to follow the dastardly demon in its footsteps and effectively become its shadow as we followed it from room to room. By the time the burglar had reached the attic, frustration was clearly starting to set in, for the pace became more frantic, the breathing more erratic, and the occasional curses being uttered more frequent and vociferous. All in all, I had the impression that this burglar, contrary to the ones we had caught last night, wasn't simply out to grab the nearest valuable item they could find. Clearly, he or she was looking for something very specific.

We heard the burglar rummaging around in the attic and exchanged curious glances.

"What is he doing up there?" asked Harriet.

"Maybe he lost something?" Dooley suggested. "And now he wants it back."

"What's taking Brutus so long?" asked Harriet with a touch of irritability.

"Like he said, it's not easy waking up a human," I said. "Once they enter deep sleep, their brain will hold on to it, resisting the urge to wake up."

"Pretty soon this burglar will come down and escape," she said. "And then what?"

I glanced at the stepladder that reached into the attic. It was one of those contraptions that you have to pull down and that operates on a powerful spring mechanism, which made me wonder... I touched a paw to the ladder and found that it easily yielded to pressure. I gave it another shove, a little more forceful this time, and lo and behold: it suddenly seemed to fold in on itself, and with a sort of snapping movement, retracted and slammed shut, flush against the ceiling.

"Now look what you've done!" said Harriet. "You broke it!"

"I don't think so," I said. "This is how these things work sometimes."

"You locked up the burglar, Max," said Dooley. "That's brilliant!"

Harriet gaped up at the ceiling, where we could hear the burglar trying to operate the stairs and failing. "Well, I'll be damned," she said. "Max, I think you just trapped the burglar."

"Looks like I did," I said, quite surprised myself.

"This thing is a health hazard," Harriet decided. "Imagine Holly being up there and one of her kids messing around with the ladder. She'll never be able to get down."

"Yeah, I agree it's not the world's best design," I said. "But at least for now, it suits our purpose perfectly."

It took another fifteen minutes or so before the cavalry arrived in the form of Odelia, Chase, and about half a dozen police officers. And as they all gathered on the landing, looking up at that trapdoor, Chase loudly yelled, "Police! Come out of there with your hands in the air!"

"Babe, he can't get out of there," Odelia pointed out. "He's stuck."

"Oh, right," said Chase, who looked a little bedraggled. So did Odelia, by the way, as if she had just stepped out of bed, which effectively she had, and so had her husband.

The police officers had all drawn their weapons and stood aiming them at the ceiling. Chase then grabbed hold of the piece of string that dangled from the ceiling and gave it a goodish yank. The door unlocked and dropped down, the ladder extended, and as we all looked up, we found ourselves staring into the face of... Norma Parkman!

CHAPTER 25

*N*orma had been placed under arrest for the crime of breaking and entering into another person's home under the cover of darkness. Looking at the butcher's wife now as she was being interviewed by Chase at the police station, she offered a pitiful sight. Without her makeup, her otherwise lustrous hair hanging like a curtain along her head, she looked decidedly less glamorous than she had before.

"No, I still haven't told Mikel about the affair," she said as she sat slumped in her chair across from Chase and Odelia. "I know I should have, but I simply couldn't bring myself to do it. So I thought I'd try and get back that phone myself, that way Holly had no evidence of the affair, and if she told Mikel, I could say she was making the whole thing up as she hates her neighbors. Which she does, by the way."

"Can you blame her?" said Chase. "All the neighbors knew about the affair, and yet they decided to conspire together to keep Holly in the dark, effectively siding with you in trying to hide the affair from your lover's wife."

"I never asked them to," said Norma. "I guess they simply liked me better than they did her."

"Because you've been living there all your life, and Holly is a newcomer."

Norma hung her head. "I know I shouldn't have done it, but if Mikel found out... And besides, this is old news. Eric died four years ago, so why should I suffer now for something that happened such a long time ago?"

"What I was wondering, Mrs. Parkman," said Odelia, "is what you meant by the phrase 'untold riches.' Which is what you promised Antoine would find at Holly's house."

She shrugged. "I had to tell that man something. I couldn't pay him a lot, so I just figured..."

"That he would help himself to whatever he needed," Chase said.

"Holly has been very mean to me," said Norma quietly.

"You slept with her husband!"

"I know. I probably shouldn't have done it, but Eric wasn't an innocent victim in all of this. He wanted it just as much as I did. In fact, he was the one who flirted with me. And since he was a very handsome man..." She sighed. "Still, I know it was wrong of me, especially since he'd just become a father for the second time, and Holly was in the hospital. It felt wrong, but also right. Oh, I don't know. You have to understand that Eric Mitchell was a very persuasive person. When he wanted something, he really went for it."

"So O'Neil went in search of Eric's phone," said Chase, "and took his friend Toby Grave along with him. He didn't find it, so you asked him to return a second night in a row."

"I already told you that wasn't me. When I met Antoine in the park and he told me he couldn't find the phone, even though he had looked everywhere, I figured that was it. Either I'd hired an incompetent burglar, or Holly had hidden the phone somewhere else. Either way, that was the last time I spoke to Antoine."

"You didn't pay him to break in again?"

She shook her head. "He didn't seem interested either. Said he'd found the riches I had promised, and he thanked me. Told me a lot of stuff about fate and destiny and all of that. And then he showed me a picture he had found in the attic. It showed Holly and her siblings when they were little, along with their mom and dad. For some reason, Antoine seemed very excited about the picture, as if it was the greatest treasure he had encountered. I couldn't make head nor tail of his babbling and just thought he was high, which he often was, apparently."

"So why did he return to the Mitchell place two nights ago?"

"Beats me. When I heard that his body had been found, I was as surprised as anyone. I definitely never asked him to go back. I thought maybe he felt bad that he hadn't found what I had sent him in there for and decided to give it another shot."

"So you didn't kill him?"

"Me? Are you nuts? Why would I kill the guy?"

"Because he was blackmailing you? You had promised him untold riches and instead all he found was some old photo album. I think it was his way of letting it be known you had cheated him, and now he wanted money in exchange for his silence. And since you didn't have any money to give him, you decided to get rid of him once and for all. So you agreed to meet Antoine at Holly's place and killed him."

"I already told you I was home with Mikel that night. I mean, I would never... I don't even own a gun, much less know how to handle one. You have to believe me, detective, I didn't kill Antoine. I paid him to break in for me, I admit that. And I broke in tonight, hoping to finally lay my hands on that stupid phone with those stupid messages I should never have sent in the first place, but I never murdered anyone. The only thing I'm guilty of is my affair with Holly's husband, but that's it."

I was inclined to believe her, and clearly Odelia was too. But Chase kept harping on the fact that it was too much of a coincidence that Antoine would have broken into Holly's house on Norma's instigation and then the second night had been killed there. But no matter how hard he tried, Norma remained firm in her insistence that she wasn't guilty of that particular crime.

In the end, Chase decided to charge her with burglary and also with conspiring to commit burglary with O'Neil and Grave. I think he knew he couldn't make the murder charge stick. And besides, he already had Chris Goldsworthy and Julio West locked up on that charge.

"Looks like the lockup is filling up fast," said Brutus.

We were in the little room that offered a good view of the interview room. Next to us, the Chief had also been watching, since this case had received a lot of attention and it was imperative that the murder was solved and the culprit charged, arraigned, and sentenced.

"So how many people have been arrested so far?" asked Harriet.

"Well, Chris Goldsworthy and Julio West for human trafficking," I said, "and also for the murder of Antoine O'Neil. Toby Grave for burglary. And now Norma Parkman for burglary and conspiracy to commit burglary."

"Great," said Harriet. "Looks like that's all the cases solved. And in record time, no less! And all thanks to us, you guys." She glanced at the Chief, who stood fingering his fleshy chin. "You can say thank you now, Uncle Alec!" she said.

But of course, Odelia's uncle didn't respond. Instead, he sort of stared before him with unseeing eyes, his mind clearly miles away. Then when Odelia and Chase finally joined us, he turned to his detective. "Are you sure the Parkman woman didn't murder that bum? I think she could have done it."

"We already have Goldsworthy and West for the murder," Chase reminded his superior. "And they look like better suspects than Norma Parkman."

"I'm not sure," the Chief confessed. "I just spoke to Goldsworthy's lawyer, and he insists his client had nothing to do with the murder. He's prepared to confess to the other charges, but not the murder."

"Of course, he would say that," said Chase with a shrug. "But I think that man's as guilty as they come. Whereas Norma Parkman is only guilty of one thing: falling for the wrong man and getting herself into a heap of trouble as a consequence."

"Hmm," said the Chief, but he clearly wasn't buying what Chase was selling. "Talk to the husband," he advised. "Search the Parkmans' place and the butcher shop. We still haven't found the murder weapon."

"We were going to talk to Mikel Parkman," said Chase, "but with one thing and another we haven't gotten around to it yet."

"Maybe he isn't as in the dark as his wife seems to think. Maybe he found out about the affair and about his wife's extracurricular activities trying to retrieve that phone and decided that she was having an affair with O'Neil."

"That was our first thought," said Chase. "But Norma vehemently denies it and I think she's telling us the truth where O'Neil is concerned. The man was a drunk, an addict, and had been living on the street for twenty-five years. Norma wouldn't have been attracted to a guy like that."

"Just talk to the husband, will you? Though I have to say the Goldsworthy angle sure looks appealing. That type of guy would do anything for money."

And since our business for the night was done, Odelia thanked us profusely, and then proceeded to take us home to get some rest. Chase would wrap up at the precinct and follow in due course. All in all, it had been a fruitful night, and I had high hopes we had all the suspects behind bars at this point.

Though one thing did give me pause: that picture Antoine O'Neil had found.

For some reason, I thought that just might be important.

So on the drive home, I asked Odelia if the picture had been found on O'Neil's person, but she said it hadn't, and also not amongst his personal belongings that were retrieved from the park.

Which struck me as very odd indeed.

CHAPTER 26

I have to admit I was looking forward to a nice long nap. But when we arrived home, it soon became clear that it wasn't to be. For when we entered the backyard, I was surprised by the number of cats present there. Shanille was there, but also Clarice, Kingman, Buster, and pretty much all of our friends from cat choir. Oddly enough, even Fifi and Rufus were there, and also Roger Moore, Babette, Melvin, and a lot of dogs I had never seen before. All in all, our backyard looked more like the local kennel than our usual peaceful haven of delight!

"Max, we did it!" said Shanille the moment we arrived on the scene. "We collected all of cat choir and all of dog choir, and we're going to hold our rehearsals here from now on!"

I have to admit I goggled at her. "But…"

"We had to find a solution," Kingman explained. "Now that the park is off limits due to the infestation of those voracious cat eaters, the only safe place for now is your backyard. I mean, they won't follow us here, not with Chase present, and Odelia. Not to mention the leader of the watch committee!"

"But, but…"

"Consider this an honor, Max," said Shanille warmly. "The honor to host cat choir falls on your house, and I can see how glad you are!"

"But, but, but…"

"He's getting all emotional," said Kingman with a smile.

"Exactly like I knew he would."

"Is cat choir relocating to my backyard?" asked Harriet. Contrary to me, she seemed over the moon at this sudden change.

"Yes, it is!" said Shanille. "And if it's up to me, this will be our new home base from now on—indefinitely!"

"What safer place to rehearse than the home of a cop?" Kingman reiterated.

Odelia didn't seem particularly excited about the prospect of hosting cat choir—or dog choir, for that matter. "You're not going to make too much noise, are you?" she asked. "Some of our neighbors don't like noise."

"She's referring to my human," Fifi said with a grin. "Kurt hates it when we sing. He thinks it's just a lot of noise."

"He's probably right," said Clarice. "Most of you can't sing."

The slur was swept aside in the general excitement of having found a location where we all would be safe from now on.

"I don't believe this," said Brutus, as he took me aside. "You know what this means, don't you, Max?"

"A lot of trouble?"

"A lot of cats using our litter boxes and eating our food! They'll think this is one big party, and we're the hosts, and hosts are expected to provide food and drinks for their guests." He gave me a look of distinct concern. "Our litter boxes weren't designed for a couple of dozen cats, Max! Or our food supply!"

"We could tell them to do their business in Blake's field," I suggested.

"Yeah, we could, but you know what cats are like. They'll simply ignore us and use our litter boxes anyway!" He sighed. "This is a disaster, I just know it. And it's all Chris Goldsworthy's fault!"

Mr. Goldsworthy was quickly becoming the bane of all of Hampton Cove. His megalomaniacal plans to become rich were hurting us all—people and pets alike.

"Okay, so maybe let's go with it for now," I suggested.

"There's not much else we can do, I guess."

"And then when the park is open for business again, we'll relocate."

"Didn't you hear what Shanille just said? She wants us to host cat choir indefinitely from now on—work under the protection of Chase! As if he's the King of Hampton Cove and grants everyone his royal protection or something."

Dooley had joined us. "Isn't this neat, you guys? Now we don't even have to go to the park anymore. We can join cat choir in the comfort of our own home!"

"Our home won't be comfortable for very long," Brutus pointed out.

Dooley hadn't considered this, and when Brutus repeated his lament about our food and litter boxes, our friend made a face. "But I don't want them to eat all of my food, Max! Or use my litter box."

"We'll simply tell them to use Blake's Field," I repeated.

But then Shanille called us to order and announced that the rehearsals would commence. And when Fifi stepped up next to her and said they would hold a combined rehearsal of cat and dog choir together, the excitement reached a fever pitch. Except possibly with our neighbors. The moment dozens of cats and dogs launched into their first song of the evening, windows were opened on all sides, and the flabbergasted faces of our neighbors became visible, staring at the spectacle in wide-eyed wonder.

It wasn't long before the first shoes whizzed through the air and hit their mark. Though when one of Kurt's sneakers hit Fifi in the rear, and she barked loudly in protest, her owner expressed his regret by loudly yelling, "I'm sorry, darling! But what the hell are you doing with all of those cats?!"

"I'm expressing my art!" she yelled back.

I don't think he got it, though, for he shook his head and retreated inside, firmly closing the window as he did.

The Trappers seemed more amenable to the artistic ambitions of their canine charge. When Rufus launched into a nice solo, Ted and Marcie even applauded, extending their support. At the end, Rufus took a bow and seemed pleased as punch.

All in all, it didn't go all that badly. At least I didn't think it did. Until the first police car pulled up in front of our pleasant little home, followed by many more. Apparently, plenty of neighbors hadn't merely expressed their criticism by dispensing with their footwear, but also by calling 911 to lodge a noise complaint. Before long, Odelia was engaged in conversation with the girls and boys in blue, negotiating a truce between herself and the neighborhood and requesting us to stand down for now, lest she and her family were driven out of town feathered and tarred.

And thus ended the first joint rehearsal of cat and dog choir in our backyard. It wasn't a great success by all accounts, but it certainly was memorable. Though perhaps not worth repeating.

CHAPTER 27

*O*ur backyard had emptied out, and one of the last stragglers was Babette. So I told her about Norma Parkman and the break-in. She didn't seem surprised.

"Mikel Parkman is not an easy guy, so I can understand why Norma wouldn't want to come clean about the affair. Even going so far as to commit a crime to cover up what happened."

"Chase and Odelia will talk to Mikel in the morning, and they will tell him what happened and what his wife has been up to."

I could imagine the conversation wouldn't be an easy one, and I sincerely hoped Mikel wouldn't pick up a butcher's knife or an axe and attack my humans. Then again, maybe they'd invite him to the police station for the chat so he would be removed from his arsenal of potentially deadly weapons he employed every day with practiced ease. And while he was being interviewed, other police officers would search the house he and Norma shared and also the shop, in search of the gun that killed Antoine and potentially other indications that Norma wasn't the innocent woman she claimed to be.

"The odd thing is that Antoine O'Neil found a picture of Holly's mom and dad and her siblings, and he seemed to attach a great deal of value to it. Even claiming it was the untold riches Norma had told him he'd find. And even more oddly, the picture has since gone missing. Any idea what that could be about?"

Babette thought for a moment, then shook her head. "No idea, Max, I'm sorry. Maybe the picture reminded him of his own family? Didn't you mention that O'Neil lost his wife and kids in some tragic event? And that's how he ended up losing everything and living on the street? Maybe you should dig a little deeper into that."

"Good advice," I said. Though I was sure Chase hadn't neglected that particular angle and had asked one of his colleagues to do a background check on the man. Clearly, it hadn't thrown up any leads, or else he would have told us. "So how are you holding up?"

"Oh, I'm fine," Babette assured me. "Holly's mom and dad are so happy that their daughter decided to return home, even if only for a little while, and especially that they get to spend time with their grandkids. And of course, Sylvester and Ruby are loving every minute of it, since their grandparents are determined to spoil them rotten."

"And Holly?"

"Still shaken, but I think she'll be all right. The events of the past couple of days have made her think that maybe she should sell the house and move away. But the kids won't hear of it. They'd have to miss their friends from school, and they don't want that. So she's still divided on how to proceed."

"She could move to a different neighborhood," I suggested. Now that both her next-door neighbors had been arrested, maybe her relationship with her neighbors would become even more untenable if they all sided with Chris and Julio and blamed Holly for the arrests. Though I couldn't see how they would. After all, their guilt was obvious, and clearly Holly was the injured party here. But then human psychology works in mysterious ways, and they might twist things around to such an extent that they would end up blaming her instead.

"I think it will be fine," said Babette. "In the end, she'll do the right thing. Or maybe we'll end up staying at her parents' house for a while, until things become clearer." She gave me a smile. "I wanted to thank you, Max, for all that you've done. You and your friends."

"Oh, well, we didn't do much," I said. "Mostly Odelia and Chase did everything."

"No, but if you hadn't staked out the house, Norma wouldn't have been arrested. So thank you for that."

Dooley had joined us, and he didn't look so happy. "We didn't find the ghost, though," he told Babette. "We tried two nights in a row, but the ghost wouldn't show up."

"Which probably means there is no ghost," Babette pointed out. "Which is all to the good, Dooley. No ghost means we can move back in with no problem."

"I know," he said, "but I would like to have seen the ghost. You hear so much about the creatures, and I would have liked to be the first to actually lay eyes on it."

"I'm not sure how happy you would have been," said Babette. "Ghosts aren't always the pleasant fluffy creatures they're made out to be, Dooley. Ghosts can be mean and vengeful, and they can do some real damage if you let them."

"You think?" asked Dooley, staring at the tiny Chihuahua with dismay.

"Absolutely. So I think you had a lucky escape, Dooley. If I were you, I'd be grateful that you didn't meet a ghost, not disappointed."

"Oh, dear," said our friend, having blanched a little beneath his fur.

"So next time, don't go looking for danger, you hear? Danger has a habit of finding you, so don't tempt fate."

She seemed to have momentarily forgotten that it was actually she who had 'hired' us to find this elusive ghost and get rid of him. Then again, I guess even dogs can suffer from a selective memory.

"That's such good advice," said Dooley earnestly. "Thank you so much, Babette."

"You're welcome. And now I have to go. Otherwise, Holly will be the one phoning 911 and reporting me missing."

"Do you want us to escort you home?" I asked.

"Be careful," said Dooley. "The streets are teeming with cat eaters, and if they like cat meat, they're bound to like dog meat too!"

She smiled. "If I see a dog eater, I'll simply pop into one of the neighboring gardens and make myself scarce. I'm so tiny they probably won't even see me!"

We said goodbye to our canine friend, and then it was time to finally retire for the night. Chase had returned from the police station and was already in bed with Odelia. A pleasant calm had descended over the neighborhood, and I, for one, was glad for it. These social gatherings are all well and good, but nothing beats a nice prolonged nap. And I'd just put down my head when a thought occurred to me. It had to do with that picture. And try as I might, it wouldn't let go!

CHAPTER 28

*B*abette arrived home safe and sound, and despite her airily dispensed reassurances that she wasn't concerned, she still breathed a sigh of relief the moment she passed through the pet door and was home again. Even though she was tiny and didn't have a lot of meat on her bones, an enterprising person with a big stomach might still consider her a nice tasty snack!

The moment she tripped into the bedroom and snuggled up to her human, she was gratified to find that Holly also seemed extremely relieved to see her.

"And where did you go off to, huh?" she said. "Don't tell me, having fun with your friends again?"

"I did," she said. "A lot of fun with a lot of friends." With that, she settled in for the night and soon was sound asleep.

Morning broke with a surprise: the doorbell rang insistently and incessantly. Babette hopped down from the bed and made her way downstairs to see who could be there at this early hour. Holly's mom was already up, answering the door. To Babette's surprise, it was none other than Detective Kingsley and his wife, along with Max and Dooley!

"What are you guys doing here?" she said. Then she sagged a little. "Oh, no. Has something else happened? Not more bad news, please."

"I'm afraid so," Max announced.

"Better take a seat, Babette," Dooley added.

Babette tripped into the kitchen and sank down on her favorite spot: her basket located near the window, which offered the perfect view of the backyard. "Okay, shoot," she said, even though she wished this stream of bad news would simply stop. Hadn't they suffered enough already?

"Okay, so do you remember I mentioned a picture that Antoine O'Neil stole?" asked Max.

"I do, yes. A picture of Holly and her brothers and sisters."

"And their parents."

"Uh-huh. So?"

"So this whole business with the picture simply wouldn't let go of me, and then I remembered something else. Something you once told us. That Holly's parents went through a rocky patch early in their marriage."

"They did. But they've since found each other again and are very happy now."

"So I thought and thought, and finally decided to wake up Odelia again."

"She wasn't happy," Dooley commented.

"I asked her if the background check on Antoine O'Neil had thrown up something useful. Turns out that Antoine was raised by a single mother, a drug addict, who died when he was young, and Antoine ended up living with his aunt and uncle. Then in later years, he worked as a banker for a while, got addicted himself, and ended up losing his job, his house, his family, and living on the street."

"His family died?"

"No, his wife left him because of his habit. The odd thing

is that Antoine's mother was originally from Hampton Cove, and Antoine was also born here."

"But no dad."

"Well, he had a dad, but never knew the man. His mother did have a picture of the guy and passed it on to her son, who kept it all this time in a locket around his neck. A picture of his mom and dad, and also of his own family."

"I didn't know about the locket."

"That's because the locket went missing. Toby Grave saw it, though. Antoine once showed it to him. But after Antoine was murdered, whoever killed him also took the locket. And now we know why."

She eyed the big orange cat with interest. "Why?"

"Because Antoine recognized his dad in Holly's family picture."

Babette blinked. "Come again?"

Max pointed to the breakfast nook, where his humans were now seated across from Holly, her mom, and dad. "That man is Antoine's dad... and also his killer."

That man now gave Odelia and Chase a look of concern. "I don't understand."

"Yes, what are you talking about?" asked Holly. "You're accusing my dad of... what, exactly?"

"Antoine O'Neil was hired by Norma Parkman to retrieve your husband's phone," Odelia explained. "He didn't find it because you put it in your safe at the bank. But what he did find was an old photo album full of pictures from when you were little. And in those pictures, he clearly recognized the man his mother had always told him was his dad. He kept a picture of the man in a locket around his neck, and when he compared the pictures, he must have immediately seen the similarities. Which is why he told Norma that he had indeed found untold riches, namely the identity of his father."

"What happened, Charlie?" asked Chase. "Did Antoine contact you out of the blue? Tell you that he was your son?"

Charlie was shaking his head. "I don't know what you're talking about, I really don't."

"How old was Antoine O'Neil?" asked Holly's mom.

"Forty-two."

"We had a wobble," she explained. "Me and Charlie. Early in our marriage. I was pregnant with Mimi, and we had a fight over something I can't even remember now, and we ended up splitting up for a couple of months. Eventually, we found each other again, but I always suspected that Charlie had an affair while we were apart." She eyed her husband with concern. "Did you have an affair with Antoine O'Neil's mother, Charlie?"

"Of course not! How could you even think that?"

"Dad would never do such a thing," Holly said adamantly.

"Never," her dad confirmed. "That time we were apart was the worst time of my life. I prayed every day that God would find a way to reunite us, and somehow He did, and I've been grateful every day since."

"It's not difficult to ascertain whether you were Antoine's father, Charlie," said Chase. "A DNA test will prove beyond a doubt whether you had an affair with his mom and out of that relationship, a son was born."

"Antoine was convinced that you were his dad," said Odelia. "So what did he want, Charlie? Did he ask for money? Did he threaten to tell Holly?"

Charlie had been shaking his head all the while, but it was clear he wasn't going to win this particular battle. DNA results would prove one way or another whether he was lying right now, and Babette could tell that Holly and her mom were already starting to waver. She turned to Max. "Did he kill his own son?"

Max nodded. "He did."

Holly must have put two and two together, for she produced a tiny gasp of shock. "Dad," she said. "What did you do?!"

Which is when Charlie turned to her and said, "I had to, darling. That drug addict left me no choice."

Bethany was too shocked to respond, but Holly wasn't. "Dad, you didn't!"

Charlie heaved a deep sigh and wrung his hands. He didn't meet his daughter or his wife's eyes. "He approached me when I stepped out of the house to go for a walk. He must have been watching me, for suddenly he was there. I hadn't even seen him. He showed me his locket and the picture he stole from Holly and told me he was my son and he could prove it. Then he said he would tell Bethany if I didn't pay up. I was too shocked to think straight, so I told him he had to give me some time. He said he wanted fifty thousand, and if I gave it to him, he wouldn't bother me again. But I could tell that wouldn't be the end of it. He felt he'd hit the mother lode, and he would keep coming back for more. He said as much, figuring he was on to a good thing and that he was so happy to finally meet. So I said I'd think about it, and I did. But I quickly decided I wasn't going to fall into his trap. I did meet his mom but there was no affair. Not like Antoine seemed to think. I was feeling very low at the time, and she worked at the motel where I stayed after Bethany and me broke up. She was sweet and kind, and we slept together a couple of times. Then she started asking me for money, and I decided I'd made a big mistake and ended things with her. She phoned me after Bethany and I reconciled, but I told her I couldn't see her anymore. I figured that was the end of that."

"She never told you that she was pregnant?" asked Chase.

"She didn't. Though I have to admit I stopped taking her calls."

"And then forty-two years later, suddenly Antoine O'Neil shows up and starts blackmailing you."

He nodded. "I didn't know what to do. On the one hand, I didn't want to give that man any money, but on the other hand, I didn't want him to tell Bethany or the kids either. So in the end, I decided that maybe..." His voice faltered, and he rubbed his face. "I decided to end things once and for all."

"Oh, Charlie," said his wife.

"Where did you get the gun?"

"I got it from a friend. He works at the shooting range, and when I told him I needed a gun, he gave it to me, no questions asked. He said it had never been used in a crime and so it was clean. Any bullets fired from that gun couldn't be traced back to it. I used it once, then returned it to him."

"So you arranged to meet Antoine and then shot him? But why at your daughter's house?"

"That was his idea. He said he was looking for Eric's phone and wanted me to find it for him. Said he could get good money for that phone. I had the impression he was going to use it in another blackmail scheme."

"He was going to blackmail Norma?" asked Odelia.

Charlie nodded. "Said she was desperate to lay her hands on that phone. So he would give it to her for a price—or to her husband if she didn't pay up."

"So you both showed up there and..."

"I shot him, then got out of there as fast as I could. I figured you'd think one of his drug-addict friends had shot him. Falling out amongst thieves kind of thing."

"We did think that," Chase admitted.

"What about those Legos?" asked Odelia. "That ship and the poem Holly's husband wrote."

"I didn't know anything about that, I swear," said Charlie. "I only heard about it after the fact. All I can think is that Antoine must have stolen it from us. We keep some of Eric's

Legos in the attic, so my best guess is that after he broke into Holly's place and discovered that picture, he broke in here as well and found those Legos and decided to give them as a present to Holly's kids. My impression was that the man wasn't right in the head. He seemed fascinated with our family, but in a twisted sort of way. Called Holly his long-lost sister, and talked about all the things we were going to do as a family once I'd introduced him to her and to the kids. Which is why I knew we'd never get rid of this guy. If I'd known he had brought Eric's Legos, I would have removed them. But after I shot him, I just ran."

"I don't believe this," said Holly. "You shot and killed a man in my house, Dad. Your own son!"

Charlie looked up sharply. "Hey, that man was no son of mine!" he said with some heat. "He was a lowlife piece of—"

Just then, his grandkids walked into the kitchen, attracted by all the noise. Ruby toddled up to her mom while Sylvester stood eyeing the strange scene with interest. "Who are these people, Mom?" he asked. "And why is Granddad shouting?"

Which is when Charlie Williams broke down into tears, and so did Bethany.

And Babette had a feeling things would never be the same again.

CHAPTER 29

*I*t was barbecue time in our backyard, and I'm happy to say only our immediate family was present. No members of cat choir or dog choir had shown up unannounced, and frankly I hoped it would stay that way. I love my friends from cat choir dearly, but having them over for dinner every week would simply be too much. In spite of our repeated pleas to use Blake's Field for their bathroom breaks, our friends had still managed to use our litter boxes, leaving them and the area surrounding them soiled beyond comprehension. I had a sneaking suspicion that more than a few dogs had also used this opportunity to do their business where it shouldn't have been done. Our humans had spent quite a lot of time having to clean up the mess and had expressed a fervent wish that this was the first but also the last time they played host to what had felt like the entirety of Hampton Cove's cat and dog population.

Tex was manning the grill, assisted by his able-bodied son-in-law, Chase, and his brother-in-law, Alec, though as far as I could tell, the assistance consisted mainly of helping

Tex down a few beers and shooting the breeze about this and that.

The four of us were on the porch swing, taking some well-deserved R&R after the quite shocking events of the last couple of days—and nights.

Also in attendance were Charlene, who was telling Marge, Odelia, Gran, and Scarlett all about the operation to return the park to its former glory by putting all of its temporary residents into shelters located in different parts of the state.

"So far, so good," she said as she kept her fingers crossed. "Looks like they're staying away for now, which is a good thing, seeing as we were getting more and more complaints from concerned citizens about their kids being confronted by scenes of drug abuse and people being harassed by strangers begging them to part with their cash. Things have returned to normal now, and a good thing, too."

"What about Christopher Goldsworthy?" asked Marge. "Will he be facing charges?"

"Absolutely," said the Mayor. "Him and his associate, Julio West. I can't imagine what those two were thinking. Although, actually, I can. They probably had dollar signs in their eyes when they thought up this crazy scheme."

"To destroy your own town just so you can make some money," said Scarlett, shaking her head. "What a sad state of affairs."

"I knew they were a sad excuse for a neighborhood watch," said Gran. "Didn't I tell you, Scarlett?"

"You did."

"Good thing we arrested them," said Gran with satisfaction. "And to think we got a lot of flak from Alec while we were doing all of you a favor!"

"To be fair, Alec didn't know at the time that

Goldsworthy and West were actively involved in this people trafficking scheme," Charlene pointed out.

"He should have known!" said Gran. "I knew, and why? Because I follow my instincts. Always follow your instincts!" she instructed her audience. "You can never go wrong that way."

"At least we found Antoine O'Neil's murderer," said Marge. "Sad business, though. Holly Mitchell has already suffered so much, and now with her dad being arrested..."

"The hits just keep on coming," Odelia confirmed with a nod.

"So is she going to return to her own house now?" asked Marge.

"Yes, she is. Turns out that the neighbors all came together for an impromptu meeting, and they decided that they've treated Holly horribly. She was never the culprit, and it was actually they who behaved badly. So they decided to send a representative to Holly and to tell her that they feel terrible and want to apologize to her for the things that happened."

"Who was the representative?" asked Marge.

"Mae West."

"The one with the cherry tree?"

"One and the same. Julio never told her about what he was up to, and she feels just as betrayed by her husband as Holly does over the role her dad played in the murder of Antoine O'Neil. And Chris Goldsworthy's wife also paid her a visit to apologize. She also had no idea what Chris and his good buddy Julio were up to and says she feels terribly ashamed. Even Mark Cooper has decided to end the parking space war and has offered a truce, which Holly has gratefully accepted."

"What's going to happen to Norma Parkman?"

"She will be charged, though she'll probably get off with a

suspended sentence and a fine. I think she's more afraid of her husband's reaction than going to prison, but we talked to Mikel, and he seems to understand that his wife has been under a great deal of pressure lately. He paid her a visit, and I think they'll get through this episode. There's still a lot of love there."

Marge had disappeared into the house and now returned with a gigantic cherry cake. "A present from Holly," she announced. We all laughed. "And the cherries were donated by Mae West herself."

"Looks like the cherry war is also over," said Charlene with a smile.

"When are they going to bake a turkey cake?" asked Dooley. "I mean, cherries are fine, but turkey is better, right?"

"I'm not a big fan of cherries," Brutus admitted.

"Me neither," I said.

"Turkey is the cherry on top of the cake," Harriet said, becoming philosophical.

"There's something that still bothers me," Charlene now revealed.

"What's that?" asked Odelia.

"Well, Eric Mitchell's accident four years ago. Was it really an accident?"

"It was," Odelia confirmed. "Turns out he and Norma were sexting, causing Eric to become reckless and crash his car into that ditch. If he had been more careful, he would still be alive today."

"If he hadn't had the affair with Norma while his wife was having their baby in the hospital," said Marge, "then he would still be alive."

"Men," said Gran. "They're all the same."

"Well, not all of them," Charlene said. "I have to say I lucked out in that department."

"Me too," Odelia said with a smile.

"And me," Marge added.

They all turned to their partners gathered around the grill. Uncle Alec, Chase, and Tex were still shooting the breeze.

"I wonder what they are talking about," said Marge.

"No doubt something important about the case," Odelia imagined.

"Or some great new idea for our town," Charlene suggested.

"Or a medical breakthrough," Marge marveled. "Worthy of the Nobel Prize."

And since cats are by nature curious animals, we decided to hop down from our swing to have a listen.

"A pimple is not the same thing as a wart," Chase was saying. "There's a big difference, Alec."

"So how do you get rid of them?" asked Uncle Alec.

"If it's a wart," Tex said, "you freeze it or you burn it."

"What about a pimple? Can you freeze a pimple?"

"I've never tried," Tex confessed. "But in theory, you should be able to reduce its size. You remove the inflammation, you see, making it go away."

"The reason I ask," said Uncle, "is I've got this pimple on my butt." And to prove to the others he wasn't lying, he proceeded to discreetly lower his pants a few inches and give us the benefit of a glimpse at his hairy behind. And lo and behold, there was indeed an angry-looking pimple there.

"If you want, I could try freezing it," Tex suggested after he had studied the pimple more closely. "Come into my office tomorrow, and we'll apply some liquid nitrogen to that thing."

Chase was giggling like a teenager. "It looks like a volcano!"

We all shared a look, shook our heads, and decided to

remove ourselves from the scene. "Men," Harriet said with a shake of her head. "They never really grow up, do they?"

"No, they sure don't," Brutus agreed.

We returned to the swing, in eager anticipation of some tasty morsels, which is when Dooley had an idea that gave us all reason for concern.

"You guys, are you sure Tex will wash his hands before handing us our portions? I mean, just look at him, checking out Alec's pimple!"

We all looked, and it did indeed take away some of our appetite to see our very own grillmeister studying his brother-in-law's hindquarters up close and personal, taking a distinct professional interest in the phenomenon.

"I'm not hungry anymore," Harriet announced.

"Me neither!" said Dooley.

"And me," said Brutus.

Then again, you never know where the hands of the people preparing the food at a restaurant have been or the servers. So maybe it's best not to give too much thought to that part of the operation. And so I closed my eyes, put the whole scene at the grill firmly out of my mind, and simply sniffed those delicious smells emanating from the grill and wafting our way. Before long, I was as hungry as I had been before, eager to partake in the feast. But when I opened my eyes again, I saw that of my three friends, there was no trace. Clearly, they had decided to remove themselves from the equation.

I shrugged. It just meant more meat for yours truly.

But when Odelia finally arrived with our portions and noticed the distinct absence of three-quarters of her feline household, she seemed both surprised and concerned.

"It's your uncle's butt that put them off their food," I explained. Of course, she didn't understand, which was all to the good since I didn't want to put her off her food as well. In the end, she decided to go in search of her cats, and since I felt bad about eating my share while my friends were possibly starving, I joined her.

We got as far as our own backyard before we spotted the three musketeers, lazily lounging on the deck.

"Aren't you guys hungry?" asked Odelia. "There's plenty of food next door for you."

"We're fine," said Brutus with a wave of his paw.

"Yeah, we're on a diet," Harriet announced.

"I'm not on a diet, but I'm not hungry," said Dooley.

Odelia frowned with concern and planted her hands on her hips. "Okay, you're going next door right now, and you're going to eat what's on your plates. Is that understood?"

Murmuring words of apology, my three friends quickly got up and returned to where they came from, single file. Odelia and I brought up the rear, and before long, we were all tucking into our plates with relish.

The odd thing about food is that it's so much tastier when eaten with others. I don't know why that is, but it's true. If I were to hazard a guess, I would say that maybe as much as fifty percent of the good taste is made up by the fact that you're enjoying your meal in the presence of your friends and family. At least for me that seems to be the case. And judging from my friends and our humans gathered around the table, I think it's safe to say it applied to them as well.

We finished our meals, lay down for a nice nap, and soon we were all fast asleep, dreaming of turkey, cherries, and cake. Though not for long.

"Max?"

"Mh?"

"Is chicken the pimple on top of the cake?"

I opened my eyes to take in my friend. "What makes you say that?"

"Well, if turkey is the cherry on top of the cake, it stands to reason that chicken is the pimple, since chickens are smaller than turkeys."

"Dooley, go to sleep," I said with a groan.

"All right, Max."

For a moment, no one stirred, then Brutus suddenly started to giggle wildly, moments later followed by Harriet.

"Is it something I said?" asked Dooley, much surprised.

"Yes, Dooley," said Brutus in between two hiccups of laughter. "It's something you said."

"It's not logical," I pointed out. "Pimples aren't fruit. Cherries are."

"Who cares about logic!" Brutus cried, wiping tears from his eyes.

"You know?" said Harriet suddenly. "I love you guys. I really do."

"Same here," Brutus confessed. "I think you guys are just great."

"I also love you guys," Dooley said warmly. "Even though I don't get the joke."

"That's just it, Dooley," said Brutus. "You never get the joke! That's what's so funny!"

"But I don't get it!"

"And that's funny!"

"But why?"

"Oh, Dooley."

How we had gone from cherries to pimples to love, I did not know. But I had to confess I also felt a sort of warm sensation in the vicinity of my heart. And if I was honest with myself, I had to admit I suddenly felt happy to be with my friends. They might be goofy, and so was our human family, but they made me happy. Maybe that's why my food tasted so good all of a sudden.

Dooley turned to me and whispered, "Did you get the joke, Max?"

"No, I didn't, buddy."

"Oh, good. I thought I was the only one."

Brutus patted him on the back. "You're all right."

For a moment, no one spoke, then suddenly Dooley piped up, "I've got an idea. Let's go ghost-hunting again tonight!"

"No!" we all cried simultaneously.

THE END

Thanks for reading! If you want to know when a new Nic Saint book comes out, sign up for Nic's mailing list: nicsaint.com/news

EXCERPT FROM PURRFECT PILLS
(MAX 72)

Chapter One

Raoul Cauvin had been working hard all morning. He had just finished the final draft of his new screenplay, and even though he couldn't be one hundred percent sure, he had a feeling this might be it. This was the masterpiece to trump all masterpieces and would turn out to be his chef d'œuvre.

He had been working on the screenplay for many months now, laboring incessantly to whip it into shape. And now, after another sleepless night burning the midnight oil, he felt he'd gotten it just right. As he closed his laptop and sat back, stretching his arms over his head and experiencing a gentle crackling in his neck and upper back, he smiled, knowing he'd managed that rare feat: to write a blockbuster movie. Nobody knows what makes one movie a hit and another a painful and costly flop, not even studio executives, directors, producers, or anyone else who shepherds a flick through the different stages of production to the final release. But Raoul knew. He had discovered the secret.

The movie industry had always fascinated him to a great

degree, and he had been its keen student for many years. What fascinated him first and foremost was trying to nail down the formula of what it took to create a blockbuster. And now he finally had it. Even though he knew he could probably make a fortune writing a book about his secret formula, he actually had an even better idea: to write a movie following the brilliant ideas as he had outlined them in his head. Then, once the movie was the surefire hit he knew it would be, he would release his book outlining how he had gone from the initial nugget of an idea to the final product and turn it into a blockbuster movie. The kind of picture people would talk about for decades. The ultimate flick that would blow all the others out of the water.

With his modest ambitions thusly outlined, he had set about creating the perfect hit movie, and now that he had finally put the finishing touches to his screenplay, he knew it was only a matter of time before it was snapped up in a bidding war between the different studios, and he would be on velvet.

"So what do you think?" he asked his dog, a French poodle answering to the name Gina Lollobrigida. "Should I send it out right now, or let it rest for a couple of days and take another look?"

Gina barked once, indicating that he shouldn't waste time second-guessing himself and simply send off his masterpiece right now.

He grinned and decided that Gina was probably right. And so he opened his laptop again, exported the screenplay in the correct format, and called up his list of agents, managers, and producers he had painstakingly collected over the past couple of months while he was slaving away on his script, engaging other wannabe screenwriters in conversations in the different groups he was a member of. He had collected a list of about a thousand names and now put them all in BCC in an email, attached his screenplay, added a few words of introduction about himself and his hit script, then hit send.

"Done," he said with satisfaction.

Gina barked her approval. She never was one for procrastination and favored quick service.

And since now all he had to do was wait until the multi-million-dollar offers started rolling in, he decided to take Gina for a walk. After all, she deserved it, as she had been more than instrumental in the creation of his script. She was, after all, one of the main characters in the story and had been an inspiration throughout.

The story revolved around a retired police officer and his dog who traipse around the country solving crimes his not-retired colleagues find impossible to solve. Through his intuitive approach to policing and with the assistance of his gifted French poodle, man and dog solve case after case, even the ones that are most baffling. In the end, they both become highly sought-after consultants and launch into a second career as private detectives, becoming the best-paid private eyes in the country.

And the secret sauce to this admittedly rather pedestrian set-up? Saul Barker, the main character in the story, can actually talk to his dog, Gina! Now that's a twist nobody would see coming, he was convinced of it. Almost as if Sherlock Holmes had a dog to assist him in solving his cases instead of Doctor Watson. And the best part was that nobody else knew about this big secret, which had come about after Saul had been struck by lightning one night, and the next thing he knew, he could talk to dogs!

Highly original, he knew, and guaranteed to find an eager audience in both mystery lovers and dog lovers alike. It just could not go wrong with this kind of premise.

He got up to grab Gina's leash from the hook near the

door. The dog immediately jumped to attention. She recognized the gesture and started running circles on the floor, then jumped up at him in anticipation. He hooked the leash onto her collar, and then they were off to the dog park. Already Raoul could see a sequel to his movie, and maybe even a complete series. There could be ten movies with the same characters, or two dozen, or maybe the series would run indefinitely! Or possibly the studio would prefer to turn it into a hit series instead. Whatever the case may be, he was on velvet, and so it was with a song on his lips and a spring in his step that he walked along the sidewalk in the direction of the dog park, where he could let Gina off her leash so she could fraternize with her fellow canine friends while Raoul thought some more about possible sequels and beyond. And merchandising, of course. Action figures of Saul Barker and his dog Gina. Games. Books. The possibilities were endless!

From time to time, he checked his phone to see how many agents and managers had already gotten back to him. Plenty had, but so far only the canned standard response that regrettably they weren't interested.

It only took one, he knew. One person who saw the amazing potential and decided to take a chance on a new and unknown screenwriter. But so far, nothing.

He took a packet of cigarettes from his pocket and lit one up. And as he stood there, nervously dragging from his cigarette, a woman sidled up to him. She was accompanied by a small dog, and soon they were chatting amiably about this and that, but mostly about their dogs. He had discovered when he got Gina that dog owners are a most talkative group of people, and that for some, having a dog is simply an excuse to go out and about and meet other dog owners. It sure gives you a great excuse to strike up a conversation since you'll always have something in common to talk about.

"So, what do you do for a living, Raoul?" asked the woman, whose name was Jill Wheeler.

"I'm a screenwriter, actually," he revealed.

"Oh, that's so interesting. Have you written anything I've seen?"

The question was one dreaded by all aspiring writers and screenwriters.

"Not yet," he said. "I'm very much in the beginning stages of my career. But I just finished a script, and I feel it's probably the best thing I've ever written."

"That sounds intriguing," she said and gave him a curious look. "What is it about?"

As a rule, he didn't feel comfortable revealing to anyone what he had written or was working on since he was superstitious that way. But Jill had such a disarming way about her that he soon found himself telling her all about the story. He could tell it was gripping her, as he had known it would.

"And so the dog can talk to his owner?"

"That's right. That's how he's got such a high crime clearance rate."

She grinned. "The dog helps him out every time."

"He does!" He was glad that she got it so quickly. But then of course he had known that people would respond favorably to the set-up since it fully adhered to the blockbuster formula he'd created.

Jill had a great smile, he thought. When she laughed, dimples formed in her cheeks that gave her a lovely look. Odd that he had never seen her at the dog park before, but then maybe she was new in the area.

"If you like, I could send it to you," he suggested.

"Oh, I would love that."

"It looks a little weird since it's not a book but a script, but I think you'll soon get the hang of it."

"Oh, but I've read screenplays before," she said.

"You have? Not many people read screenplays." In fact, he only read them because he wrote them himself and liked to keep abreast of the trends and what his competition was up to.

"I work for Nickelodeon as a script consultant, so it's actually my job to read through all the scripts that come in and separate the wheat from the chaff."

Now wasn't that an amazing coincidence? "You wouldn't happen to know anyone interested in a story like mine, would you? I mean, it's not a kids' story, obviously, but if you work in the industry, maybe you could give me a recommendation?"

"Of course," she said, much to his amazement. "I could even do you one better. Send me your script, and I'll give it a read. And then if I like it, I'll send it on to some of my contacts. I know plenty of production companies who might be interested in your story." She gave him a radiant smile, and for a moment, he felt a little dizzy. Not only had he potentially made a breakthrough with his script, but as he took her in, he felt the early stirrings of something deep and wonderful in the vicinity of his heart.

This woman, he decided, was the full package: beautiful, smart as a whip, and she worked in the same business he was desperately trying to break into!

A sudden urge to impress her came over him, and so he decided to stray from his golden rule not to talk about his book. "I've actually been working on something else. It's a book that tries to analyze what makes a story blockbuster material. And I think I've finally cracked the code."

She gave him an appropriately impressed look. "You have? But that's great, Raoul. Could you send me a copy of the book? I would love to read it."

"It's not out yet," he said. "First, I wanted to test the theory for myself, you see."

"By writing a blockbuster movie," she said, nodding. "Good thinking. And then if you succeed, you can add the script as an addendum to the book."

"That's exactly what I was going to do!" he said, feeling exhilarated that there stood a woman so like-minded they were practically finishing each other's sentences. They loved dogs, they were in the same line of work, and they obviously shared a powerful rapport. And as a certain giddiness took hold of him, he said, "I'll send you a copy. Then you can tell me what you think."

"I'd love that, Raoul. I think it's absolutely brilliant what you're trying to achieve, and I think you'll sell your screenplay in no time."

"That's what I hope." And then turn it into a blockbuster motion picture, of course, and prove to the world that he, Raoul Cauvin, had finally cracked the Hollywood code. Which incidentally was the name of his book: 'Cracking Hollywood: How to Write a Blockbuster Movie.'

They exchanged email addresses, and he promised he would shoot her an email the moment he was back at his desk, both with the script and the book.

"Don't forget," she said. "I really want to read what you've written, Raoul."

"I won't," he promised. How could he? He'd probably never forget about this auspicious meeting.

He watched Jill walk off to take her dog home, and ambled over to a copse of trees nearby, lit a cigarette and dreamed about going to see his own movie in his own local cinema with Jill by his side. Now wouldn't that be something? They'd be eating popcorn from the same bucket and laugh at the same jokes and generally behave like any couple would. They could call their son Saul, like the character of his hit movie. And if it was a girl, Gina. And as he stood there basking in the afterglow of a wonderful conversation with an amazing lady, he checked his watch. Now what was taking so long?

Chapter Two

Parker Jones had just fed her chickens and wondered if she'd done right by them. She was a lively young woman who believed in growing her own produce, raising her own chickens, and generally reducing her ecological footprint as much as possible. In that sense, she took after her mom, who had been young in the sixties and part of the peace and love generation. And even though Parker was very much in favor of peace, she wasn't all that sure about the love bit. After all, her dad had left her mom to raise her daughter all by her lonesome, so obviously there hadn't been all that much love to share. Or maybe her dad had so much love to share he didn't think it fair to limit that vast output to one woman.

Parker watched as her chickies pecked away at the grain she had supplied with a generous hand, and a smile lit up her face. Even though they hadn't laid a single egg yet, she knew that any day now they could and would give her all the eggs she needed.

She moved over to her small patch of green located behind her lovely little home. It was a rental, but she had asked for and received permission to turn the concrete deck into a small city garden. And so she had planted a few tomato plants, some lettuce and radishes, and a few herbs, and hoped they would all produce a nice harvest at some point in the near future. She didn't think it was feasible to grow all of her own veggies, but it was a start. And if she kept this up, she might even be able to prove to her colleagues at work that homegrown tomatoes are that much juicier and tastier than the supermarket variety.

As a graphic designer, she worked for a small start-up

engaged in providing artwork for businesses that didn't have their own in-house art department. Mostly, this involved flyers and websites and such, but from time to time, she got to create some truly unique pieces. Only last week, a shoe store had commissioned artwork to liven up their shop. The theme, of course, was footwear, but she had received carte blanche to do whatever she liked. The store was small and the commission was modest, but it had given her such joy to create these unique pieces she had immediately asked her boss that if any more of such commissions came in, to ask her first. And her boss, bless his heart, had said yes!

It wasn't much, but it represented a definite stepping stone to greater success in the future.

As an art student, she had dreamed of creating her own designs, of course, but had soon realized this wasn't all that feasible. And so her mom had told her that if she wanted to get a job that would provide a decent income, she would have to compromise. And truth be told, the company she now worked for was exactly the kind of compromise she thought was suitable for her. The work was varied and challenging, her colleagues fun and quirky, and her boss was kind and open to suggestions—not the kind of corporate shark you find in some places.

All in all, she felt she had landed the perfect first job, and now if she could find the time to keep evolving her own personal style and creating her own stuff, that would be just excellent.

The doorbell jangled, and she rose from her inspection of her tomato plants to see who was at the door. Much to her surprise, it was her best friend Carol, who worked as a buyer for a big supermarket chain. Carol appeared to be on the verge of tears, and as she ushered her into her living room and instructed her to take a seat on her pink couch—in the shape of a pig—she had an inkling of what her friend was going to say.

"I left him," Carol declared sniffishly.

Parker dragged a few tissues from the dispenser and handed them to her friend, who proceeded to burst into a flood of tears. In gulps and sniffles, the whole story came tumbling out. Apparently, Carol's on-again-off-again boyfriend of five years, Tim Eltis, had cheated on her and then had the nerve to deny it.

"He lied to me!" Carol cried. "He straight-faced lied to me, Parker!"

"I know, I know," she said, as she patted her friend on the knee. For some reason, Carol kept forgiving the man, even though he had cheated on her with different women many times. He had even hit on Parker once during a Christmas party, then later denied the fact vehemently and said Parker was mistaken, and he only tried to be friendly. At first, she had hoped that Carol would finally see the light and break up with the guy, but she kept going back to him, only to have the whole cycle start up again, with the same predictable result. None of Carol's friends could make head nor tails of her behavior. She was a hard-working, extremely competent, and intelligent woman who had made a stellar career at Starmart, and yet she kept associating with this loser.

It was a mystery, and one Parker didn't think she'd ever be able to solve.

"This time it's over," Carol declared solemnly. "I won't take him back, no matter how much he begs and pleads. He's really done it this time."

"Who was it?" asked Parker, even though she wasn't really all that interested.

"A colleague from work," said Carol with a wave of the hand. "I caught them in the toilets. They were in the cubicle next to mine, and I thought I recognized his voice. So I stood on the toilet seat to take a look, and there he was: kissing Francine from accounts! Only this time, I took a picture since I knew he'd only deny the whole thing later on. But then when I showed him the picture, he said it was photoshopped and nothing happened!"

"The louse," said Parker without a lot of emotion.

"Exactly! The man is a louse. Worse, a parasite on a louse! Worse: a speck of dust on a parasite on a louse!"

Parker checked her watch. She should be getting ready for work, and if she wasn't mistaken, so should Carol. "Maybe we should get going?" she suggested.

"I quit," Carol announced, tilting her chin in a gesture of defiance.

"Oh, Carol."

"I can't work for the same company as that man! So I told him he should quit, and when he wouldn't, I said I'd quit. And you know what he did?"

"No idea."

"He laughed! Said I'd never have the guts to quit. So I walked straight to the HR department, and I told them I was quitting—effective immediately." Then she sagged a little. "They wouldn't accept my resignation, though. Said I couldn't leave them in the lurch like that—especially over such a trivial thing as Tim hooking up with Francine."

"Wait, they knew?"

"I told them," Carol admitted.

"Of course you did." Carol was the kind of person who wore her heart on her sleeve. Everyone always knew whether things between her and Tim were at an all-time high or an all-time low. In that sense, her life was like a soap opera that everyone could follow along. Or maybe a sitcom, though Carol wouldn't have agreed with that characterization.

She now sighed. "I need a different boyfriend, Parker. A

boyfriend who won't keep cheating on me with every single woman he meets."

"That's exactly right," Parker said, for once in full agreement with her friend's assessment of her complicated love life. "So why don't you join me and Frank tonight? We're going to that new place on Boulevard Square. It's supposed to be amazing."

"What new place?" asked Carol, dabbing at her eyes with the Kleenex.

"Bae Square. They serve finger food and hors d'oeuvres, and their chef is this French guy who used to work for this five-star hotel in Paris."

"So what is he doing in Hampton Cove?" asked Carol.

"No idea. But their loss is our gain. So will you join us?"

It was a high-risk proposal, of course, because chances were that Carol would tell them all about Tim all night. Then again, maybe meeting Frank would strike a match, and the two of them would hit it off together. Like most of Carol's friends, Parker never stopped trying to set her up on a date. They all fervently hoped that she would get rid of that awful Tim Eltis once and for all. And to that end, they had introduced her to a great number of eligible suitors. The only problem was that mostly Carol spent all of her first dates complaining about Tim, which proved a big turn-off for them, and as a consequence, a second date never materialized, proving to Carol that Tim was the only man for her. Then, after they had made up and things were going great again, Carol was on top of the world and forgot all about her boyfriend's tendency to stray. Until the next time. And so the cycle continued.

Parker grabbed her phone and shoved it into her backpack along with a bottle of purified water, the lunch she made herself, and her wallet. She practically hoisted her friend up from the couch. "Let's go," she said.

"If that man so much as looks at me," Carol warned.

"You'll tell him to go to hell," Parker suggested.

"Oh, I'll do more than that. I'll slap him so hard—"

"Maybe don't slap him."

"No, I'd better not."

After giving her Persian cat Minnie a peck on the head and a cuddle, she and Carol hurried out of the house and to Carol's car. Conveniently, they both worked in the same industrial park, located on the other side of Hampton Cove. Carol was at the regional headquarters for Starmart, and Parker worked for Artsy-Fartsy, the modest little start-up. Still, she wouldn't want to trade with Carol for the world. Working in such a corporate environment would probably stifle her to such an extent that she'd want to run away screaming. And vice versa, Artsy-Fartsy was certainly too low-key and quirky for Carol, who was blessed with a lot of talent and a towering ambition to become a corporate super-star. If only she'd apply that same ambition to her personal life, Parker thought.

Carol navigated the early morning traffic with practiced ease, even a touch too aggressively for Parker's taste, and before long, they had arrived at their destination. Carol dropped her off in front of her office, and she waved goodbye to her friend, but not before reminding her that they were meeting for dinner that night. At least if Carol hadn't made up with Tim before then.

Stranger things had happened.

Chapter Three

Paul Dolmen looked through his office window and saw that a bird had suddenly appeared out of the blue and started pecking at the kernels of wheat he had liberally strewn on the balcony. He smiled with satisfaction at the sight.

Boredom made his life at the company a near-constant struggle, and the idea to entertain a few of these feathered friends hadn't been his but had been supplied to him by his good friend Raoul Cauvin. The notion that he might look up from his excruciatingly tedious job as a debt adjuster and watch the birds from time to time had immediately appealed to him, both in its simplicity and the fact that it was essentially risk-free.

The debt relief company he worked for didn't condone its workforce spending precious working hours surfing the web or engaging in counterproductive extracurricular activities. If his boss caught him checking his email on his phone or scrolling through his Facebook feed, there would be hell to pay. In this day and age of the ubiquity of social media and the internet, management did its utmost to keep those productivity black holes as far removed from the work floor as possible. Cell phones had to be placed in drawers, not on top of the desk. Taking a call was permitted if it was related to an urgent family matter. A mandatory cell phone policy was part of the onboarding package for new hires. And managers were always on the lookout for employees who didn't abide by the rules.

Paul had been caught checking his Facebook feed once and had promptly been called into his supervisor's office, where he had received a verbal warning, with the understanding that his next offense would elicit a written warning, and a third meant his immediate dismissal.

So birds seemed like a much more elegant option. At least he'd have something to look at during the day apart from the numbers on his screen from people who had gotten themselves into debt and couldn't claw out of it. And he had just closed the window and returned to his desk when a shadow fell over him. He didn't even have to look up to know that his office manager Brad had joined him. The man employed the type of rubber-soled shoes that didn't make a sound and had a habit of creeping up on his employees, then hovering over them as he intently watched what they were up to.

"Those birds," Brad now said.

"Yes, sir?" said Paul.

"Is that your doing, Dolmen?"

"What do you mean?"

The manager sighed. "Someone has been feeding those birds. Why else would they suddenly show up here en masse?"

"Would you say they're en masse, sir?" he asked.

"I would, yes. So I ask you again, Dolmen: is that your doing? Are you responsible for those birds suddenly flocking to our windows en masse?"

"Well..."

The manager pinned him to the chair with one look as he leaned a little closer. "You do know that birds poop, don't you, Dolmen? They poop on the windows, they poop on the balcony, they poop on the street below."

"Is that a fact, sir?"

"It is. And it's also a fact that the entrance to the building is right beneath this balcony, causing our clients entering or leaving, as well as your own colleagues, to be bombarded with bird poop. Do you want your colleagues and the company's clients to be bombarded with bird poop, Dolmen?"

"Well, no, sir, I do not."

"Then I suggest you refrain from feeding those birds."

"Yes, sir. Of course, sir. I will, sir. Thank you, sir."

He watched the manager walk off, checking left and right at some of his other colleagues as he did. Marjorie Mooney had just taken a call, presumably from the daycare where her kids were at, and the manager stopped long enough to listen in on her conversation before giving her a warning look.

She shrugged, as if to say that it wasn't her fault that her daycare provider kept running into trouble. Brad walked on, shaking his head as he did. Clearly, the man didn't have a family of his own, or maybe his wife took care of all of that.

Paul sighed and saw how the birds picked up the final remnants of the little bag of grain he had provided that morning. Soon it would all be gone, and so would the birds, and then he'd be forced to look at nothing other than his computer screen and the backs of the heads of his colleagues, who were all busy doing the same work he was doing.

He decided to get up and get himself a cup of coffee in the small canteen. On his way back, he almost bumped into Marjorie Mooney, the same colleague who had been on the phone before. She looked as if she'd been crying, and when he asked her what was going on, she said that a drunk had walked into the daycare center where her kids were and had fallen asleep in the play corner, causing the owner to wonder if they were running a daycare or a bar.

The man had, in due course, been escorted from the scene by the police, but it made her wonder if she shouldn't stop working and stay home with her kids.

"But I can't," she said. "I have bills to pay, and we won't make it on my husband's salary alone."

He nodded in an understanding way, but then Brad caught sight of them schmoozing and directed a keen look at them. He would have said, 'Break it up,' but then he must have remembered they weren't in a prison and he wasn't a prison guard. Yet.

So Paul and Marjorie hurried right along, with Paul feeling slightly guilty at having been caught chatting with this colleague, even though he could see that the woman was clearly distraught and could have used a hug or a word of encouragement.

Back at his desk, he wondered if maybe he wouldn't be

allowed to bring a fish to work. He could buy a small fish tank and position it on the edge of his desk with a couple of fish. It sure would be nice to look at those little fishies swimming along. Or he could get a hamster and put a hamster cage on his desk. Then again, possibly that was a little too depressing, as watching that hamster run on its wheel would remind him a little too much of himself. And also, he was pretty sure that, like birds, fish and hamsters were against company policy.

All in all, he didn't have a solution for the touch of ennui that had assailed him. Mostly, he probably should work hard and eventually rise to the position of manager himself. That way, he could tell other people what to do and make sure they did it. It would definitely break the routine—even the rut he was in.

But as he sat staring out of the window, devising ways and means to liven up his work life, suddenly he caught Brad's incandescent eye, and quickly hunkered down over his computer once more, intent on suggesting ways and means for his clients to ease their burden. And as he sat thusly engrossed, suddenly a ladybug landed on his desk, glanced around for a moment to get its bearings, then started exploring his desk.

Which is when Paul got his brightest idea yet. If he couldn't have birds, or fish, or a hamster, he could keep a personal ladybug on his desk. He could train it and take it home with him in a little matchbox, and it could be his constant companion. It could be his emotional support bug. He was pretty sure there was no company policy that outlawed ladybugs. And if there was, he could simply grab the bug from his desk and tuck it inside its hiding place, and no one would be any the wiser.

It was the perfect solution to combat that dreaded ennui that threatened to derail an otherwise promising career as a debt adjuster. And as the ladybug started its exploration of Paul's keyboard, he decided to name it Mike. Though on second thought, maybe he'd better call it Alice, since ladybugs, by definition, are probably ladies, otherwise they'd be called gentlemanbugs.

"Hey, Alice," he whispered as he brought his face closer to the creature. "I'm Paul. Nice to meet you."

It could have been his imagination, but for a moment he thought that Alice fluttered her wings, as if to say, 'Great to make your acquaintance, Paul!'

ABOUT NIC

Nic has a background in political science and before being struck by the writing bug worked odd jobs around the world (including but not limited to massage therapist in Mexico, gardener in Italy, restaurant manager in India, and Berlitz teacher in Belgium).

When he's not writing he enjoys curling up with a good (comic) book, watching British crime dramas, French comedies or Nancy Meyers movies, sampling pastry (apple cake!), pasta and chocolate (preferably the dark variety), twisting himself into a pretzel doing morning yoga, going for a run, and spoiling his big red tomcat Tommy.

He lives with his wife (and aforementioned cat) in a small village smack dab in the middle of absolutely nowhere and is probably writing his next 'Mysteries of Max' book right now.

www.nicsaint.com

ALSO BY NIC SAINT

The Mysteries of Max

Purrfect Murder

Purrfectly Deadly

Purrfect Revenge

Purrfect Heat

Purrfect Crime

Purrfect Rivalry

Purrfect Peril

Purrfect Secret

Purrfect Alibi

Purrfect Obsession

Purrfect Betrayal

Purrfectly Clueless

Purrfectly Royal

Purrfect Cut

Purrfect Trap

Purrfectly Hidden

Purrfect Kill

Purrfect Boy Toy

Purrfectly Dogged

Purrfectly Dead

Purrfect Saint

Purrfect Advice

Purrfect Passion

Purrfect Model

Purrfect Slug

Purrfect Match

Purrfect Game

Purrfect Bouquet

Purrfect Home

Purrfectly Slim

Purrfect Nap

Purrfect Yacht

Purrfect Scam

Purrfect Fury

Purrfect Christmas

Purrfect Gems

Purrfect Demons

Purrfect Show

Purrfect Impasse

Purrfect Charade

Purrfect Zoo

Purrfect Star

Purrfect Ghost

The Mysteries of Max Collections

Collection 1 (Books 1-3)

Collection 2 (Books 4-6)

Collection 3 (Books 7-9)

Collection 4 (Books 10-12)

Collection 5 (Books 13-15)

Collection 6 (Books 16-18)

Collection 7 (Books 19-21)

The Mysteries of Max Big Collections

The Mysteries of Max Short Stories

Nora Steel

The Kellys

Emily Stone

Murder at the Art Class

Washington & Jefferson

First Shot

Alice Whitehouse

Spooky Times

Spooky Trills

Spooky End

Spooky Spells

Ghosts of London

Between a Ghost and a Spooky Place

Public Ghost Number One

Ghost Save the Queen

Box Set 1 (Books 1-3)

A Tale of Two Harrys

Ghost of Girlband Past

Ghostlier Things

Charleneland

Deadly Ride

Final Ride

Neighborhood Witch Committee

Witchy Start

Witchy Worries

Witchy Wishes

Saffron Diffley

An Act of Hodd

Box Set 3 (Books 7-9)

A Game of Dons

Standalone Novels

When in Bruges

The Whiskered Spy

ThrillFix

Homejacking

The Eighth Billionaire

The Wrong Woman